TWO LIFETIMES, ONE LOVE

Also by Thea Thaxton:

Dating in Cyberspace:
A book of humorous short stories about
online dating.

TWO LIFETIMES, ONE LOVE

Thea Thaxton

Ralston Store Publishing
P.O. Box 1684
Prescott, Arizona 86302

ISBN 978-1-938322-46-4

Professionally edited by:
Jennifer Hope
www.MesaVerdeMediaServices.com

Printed in the USA.

"Love and love again."
Unknown

CHAPTER ONE

THE trouble started when the chest pains appeared. His not hers. The pains started gradually and grew progressively worse. It didn't matter that Angela thought her husband Dean was too young to have chest pains. Dean was having them, and that was all that mattered. They were so frequent, though, that she thought *she* might start getting them as well, just from worrying about *him*.

All right, it wasn't fair to say that the trouble started with the chest pains. It was just one more trouble in a long list of troubles that had always dogged them, right from the beginning. Angela knew that all couples had their share of troubles during their marriage, but to her, it felt like she and Dean had *more* than their share. First it was the lawsuit in which both Dean and his partner, Kyle, were involved. It took up most of their spare time for months—finding the right lawyer, talking strategies, formulating a plan—and after all that, they lost. Then it took months for them to stop talking about it and move on.

1

When they finally got over it—or mostly over it, because neither of them ever fully recovered from the loss —the business suddenly lost a great deal of money, which meant more talks about strategy to keep it on its feet. Unfortunately, the talks didn't work. The business ultimately went under taking Dean and Kyle with it.

And those were just the *big* troubles, there were more than enough little troubles, as well. After the business went down, Dean moped around until he finally realized he had to get a job. He applied at a large corporation, but since his only job for so many years had been his own business, they deemed him qualified for only the most basic entry level position. With his own business, he had been at the top of the world. Now he was at the bottom of the heap. Angela felt so bad for him and at the same time so proud of him for stepping up and doing his part. Her salary would not support them, and their savings had nearly dried up with all Dean's business troubles. Still, she acknowledged that it took a lot of courage for him to accept that job.

Despite the entry level position, Dean excelled as usual, and within a year found himself supervisor to a willing and amiable group of people. They were not the ones causing his chest pain problem, and management wasn't the problem. It was a little of everything and maybe part of his own regret over losing his business and finding himself where he now was.

Regardless of what caused them, the chest pains grew worse. No amount of Angela trying to get him to relax or trying to get him to accept the situation helped. Not even a quick massage after work helped. Nothing helped. She tried to get him to practice yoga or meditate, but he said that was too woo-woo for him, and he refused. His stress caused Angela stress because she felt helpless to make him feel any better.

Angela knew that life could not go on the way it was with Dean getting chest pains, complaining about them, but being unwilling to do anything about them. "How about a job at the grocery store? I've heard they have great benefits."

"I'll think about it." Dean changed stations on the television and wouldn't even continue the conversation.

"How about someplace else then? Do you want to check the paper or Craigslist for other jobs?"

"I'll think about it." He didn't even look at her.

Angela gritted her teeth and walked out of the room. Sitting in the bedroom in her reading chair, she fumed. She remembered when she and Dean had first met. A friend had introduced them. Angela was just getting over a man that she was mad about who unfortunately wasn't at all interested in her. Dean was. Within weeks they were expressing their undying love for each other. But the truth will always out, won't it?

A few months after they started living together, they went out to dinner with some friends. Dean drank. A lot. And then he proceeded to regale them with how much he had liked Cindy—a woman he had been mad about who wasn't at all interested in him. For forty-five minutes he talked about Cindy, and for forty-five minutes Angela had laughed and nodded her head, all the time thinking that they were going through the same thing: in love with someone else but stuck together. It was then that she realized that their relationship was purely one of re-bounding convenience. It was a sobering realization. And here she was stuck with an unhappy and stressed man who wasn't willing to do anything about it.

3

Finally, when Dean refused to talk about getting a job anywhere else, Angela made a decision. If he wasn't willing to find another job in town, then they would either have to leave town and go somewhere else or—and it was a big or—she would have to leave him. She couldn't get around it. She wasn't willing to put up with his stress any longer. If he made an attempt to do something about it, then it would be different. But just enduring it without even trying to alleviate it or fix it was more than she could take. And the constant complaining was intolerable. Dean was just playing the victim role, and she wasn't going to continue to enable that kind of behavior.

Would he consider leaving town though? Dean loved the mountain town they lived in, and his family lived thirty miles away. He may grumble about them and their antics, but Angela knew how much he loved them. Would he be willing to leave them behind? There was only one way to find out. When he came into the bedroom to go to sleep, she broached the subject.

"Dean, what do you think about moving somewhere else? Like maybe Colorado or New Hampshire?"

* * * * *

MUNICH, GERMANY 1919/1920

In 1919, Adolf Hitler attended his first German Worker's Party meeting. In 1920, Adolf Hitler chose the swastika—the runic symbol for belonging—as the symbol for the group that he had renamed the National Socialist German Workers' Party. They called it the Nazi

Party for short.

It was also in 1920, fifty miles from Munich, that a tiny Jewish baby was born at home to unmarried parents, seventeen-year-old Miriam Levy and eighteen-year-old Aaron Abrams. They tearfully left the infant on the doorstep of the German couple they had chosen and immediately left town, never to be heard from again.

When Franz and Gerta Schluter found the tiny baby on their doorstep, it did not surprise them. They had discussed a private adoption with the young couple from another city who were friends of the family. Franz and Gerta had argued over the decision because of the baby's heritage and had never given them an answer.

The appearance of the baby made the decision for them. When Franz saw the look in Gerta's eyes as she held the baby, he knew there was no use arguing. Taking the baby from Gerta now, after she had a chance to hold her, would have far more repercussions than any danger from harboring a Jewish baby in these tumultuous times.

Gerta took the gold necklace from the baby's blanket. The golden Star of David swung in the air between her and Franz. She looked at Franz with a touch of fear in her eyes. "We must never tell anyone," she whispered, and her hand closed around the gold star. Franz clasped his two hands around his wife's hand and nodded solemnly.

Neighbors knew that the childless couple had been thinking of adopting and never questioned the new baby in the house. Franz and Gerta had the baby baptized Angelika Anna Schluter and raised her with as much love as any child could hope for.

CHAPTER TWO

ANGELA expected Dean's shoulders to tighten when she asked the questions, but instead they seemed to relax. He looked at her with a hint of a smile on his face. "Leave here? Really? I didn't think you'd ever want to leave! I know how much you love it here. You mean you'd be okay to leave?"

She let out a breath she didn't know she was holding. "I'd love to leave here, Dean. Any place to get you away from the stress."

He had been sitting on the edge of the bed taking off his shoes and socks. Now he leaned forward. "Colorado and New Hampshire both sound great!" His hand moved toward his chest, and his look turned solemn. "How soon can we leave?"

The following day was Angela's day off, and she spent the entire day on the internet researching towns where they could move. When Dean arrived home, she had six towns picked out in Colorado and five towns in New Hampshire. As they ate dinner that night, she filled him

6

in on the pros and cons of each town. He listened attentively, nodding his head, and sometimes smiling at the benefits of each one. By the time they fell asleep that night, they had picked out one town in each state. Silver Run, Colorado, and Thoreau, New Hampshire. They both fell asleep with smiles on their faces.

Angela worked the next day but arrived home before Dean. She jumped on the internet as soon as she walked through the door. It didn't take her long to order maps, newspapers, and real estate guides for each town, because she had spent most of the night awake planning what she needed to do. When she finished that, she began packing. They may not know where they were moving yet, but they were leaving for sure. She and Dean couldn't have been happier about the prospects of moving to a new place and starting their lives over again.

Every evening after work, they would pour over the information they received, comparing cost of living, housing costs, and proximity to outdoor recreation. Although Dean had been too stressed for months to go hiking, it had once been one of their favorite pastimes, and Angela hoped that he would get back into it once he relaxed a little. Finally they settled on Thoreau, New Hampshire. It was the town where Angela had once lived fifteen years before and where she and Dean had gotten married nearly ten years before. Angela loved it there, and Dean didn't mind where they ended up as long as he could leave the chest pains behind.

The excitement of their move buoyed Dean so much that his chest pains diminished. Temporarily, anyway. The one shadow that hung over their happiness was Dean's parents. Angela knew it would be that way, but she hoped that they would keep quiet for the sake of

Dean's health. They felt as worried as Angela about his constant and worsening chest pains. They had moved from Florida to Arizona two years before to be within close visiting distance of each of their three married children, including Dean.

To Angela's dismay, they not only hated the idea, but they were very vocal about it. They knew better than to say anything in front of Angela, but when they talked to Dean on the phone, they hammered him with their fears. Later, a sober Dean told her the content of their conversation.

"Dean, you have a good job now with a good company. They have great benefits. You know that."

"Mom, I'm having chest pains," he had replied. "I need to get out of there."

"Apply for another job in the company. That's not the only job. But stay with the company."

"I need to leave, Mom."

"Dean, I didn't want to say anything, but you're no spring chicken, you know. You might have trouble finding another job. You'd be a fool to give up a secure job like that."

When Dean told Angela that part of the conversation, she couldn't help giggling. Dean was thirty years old. After that comment, Dean's father took over the conversation.

"Son, you know I worked nearly fifty years on the line. I didn't like it either, but a man's got to do his job."

"It's not just that I don't like it, Dad. I've got chest pains from all the stress of it."

"Your doctor can give you something for that. You have a good secure job. You can't take the risk of not being able to find another job after you move."

"I'll find a job, Dad. Don't worry."

"Your mother knows a woman whose daughter moved to Thoreau a few years ago. She couldn't find a job. Dean, she almost took her life. So what if you can't? What happens to *you* if you can't find a job?"

When Dean told Angela about *that* part of the conversation, he said that his father sounded like he was tearing up as he talked. So that was it. Dean's parents thought that if he couldn't find a job he would kill himself. Great. What an idea to put into Dean's head.

Angela thought about the difficulty of finding a job. It was true that Thoreau wasn't a thriving metropolis, but when she lived there before, she had found a job easily. Admittedly though, she had been just a teenager. Still, the town had grown since then, meaning there were more jobs available. Putting aside the lack of jobs and the risks that entailed—and although his father had gotten so emotional—Angela still suspected that his parents' real concern was that their favorite boy-child was moving three thousand miles away. But his parents would never admit that.

After Dean finished relaying the conversation to her, Angela rested her chin in her hands and looked at him. "What now, Dean? Do we stay or do we go?"

Dean nodded his head. "We go. Yeah, we still go." But he wasn't smiling anymore.

* * * * *

GERMANY 1925

Hitler formed the Schutzstaffel, called the SS, which was the elite guard serving as his personal bodyguard.

Franz and Gerta Schluter took their precious little five-year-old girl in their arms and explained to her that she was adopted. They told her how much they loved her, and that they really were her mommy and daddy, but they deliberately left her true heritage out of the story they told her.

CHAPTER THREE

DR. Ralph Weiss looked at the clock, turned it off before it rang, and slid out of bed without disturbing his wife. After dressing, he walked down the hall and knocked softly on his daughter Carla's door. "Thanks, Dad," he heard her call sleepily. He walked past his son Curt's partially open door. Curtis had already left the house for his early morning sports practice. Dr. Weiss couldn't keep track of what sport it was.

Stepping into the kitchen, he poured a cup of coffee courtesy of Curtis. "Thank you, Curtis!" Dr. Weiss mumbled to himself. He loved his children. They were everything he had ever hoped for. No drugs, no bad behavior—sure they sometimes had attitude, but what teenagers didn't? His children were the world to him. He'd do anything for them. He scowled down the hall toward his bedroom. Even stay with *her.*

Dr. Weiss heard the swishing sound of the dog door and saw the big dog trotting toward him. "Wolfie!" He put his hands in the scruff around the dog's neck and

11

kissed him on the head. "I love you, too, Wolf! You know I do!" Wolf rubbed up against him begging for more petting. "Gotta run to work, Wolf. I'll see you later." One final stroke of the dog's shining black coat, and he stood up.

After walking outside balancing the coffee in one hand and his brief case in the other, he slid into his car. On the way to work, he smiled. He always smiled when he was out of that house. There was no peace there anymore. Curtis and Carla were usually with their friends and rarely home. The times they were home, they were on their cell phones, either talking or texting. Honestly, he didn't see the attraction, but then again, he wasn't a teenager. Dr. Weiss supposed all the kids were doing it these days.

At seven o'clock, he pulled into the parking lot—the same time he arrived every morning. He looked at the building that he owned—the grounds carefully mani-cured, the place looking inviting—and the parking lot with a smattering of cars parked at the edges. Then he took a deep breath and let the peace and serenity wash into him. This was his real home. The home he loved. The home where he belonged.

Walking into the building, he approached the first bird cage hanging from the ceiling on the left-hand side of the room. When he held his finger up to the cage, both the blue and green parakeets gently mouthed it. He whispered to them and then moved on to the next cage. As he held his finger up again, the dark blue parakeet approached, but the yellow one stayed back moving left and right nervously. It was a newer bird. His old favorite had recently died. But Dr. Weiss had confidence that the yellow parakeet would soon learn to approach him.

Only after he addressed the birds did he glance at the other side of the room where the receptionist sat behind the counter. "Good morning, Dr. Weiss," said Kelsey. He nodded to her as he walked into his office. After closing the door, he locked it. The door would stay locked until after business hours. In the days before he kept it locked all the time, too many people popped in thinking it was the restroom. He flipped the switch on his computer and proceeded into the back room to check on his patients.

Stopping at the top cages first, he took out the Chihuahua that had cataract surgery. "Looks good, little girl. No swelling, limited redness."

"Hello, Dr. Weiss." Sheila was the tech who stayed overnight with the animals. "I put drops in before I went to sleep, once in the middle of the night, and again this morning at six."

"Excellent work, Sheila. Thank you. Everybody else okay?"

"The Saint Bernard seems to be doing better. Couldn't stop wagging when I worked on the Chihuahua at three in the morning. I took her out in the back and she didn't act lethargic at all."

"Good. After I check her out, I'll call her owners to pick her up." Although he had to do it all the time, Dr. Weiss didn't like performing spays on an animal that had already gone into heat. It was just another risk that the animal didn't need. But, people being people, they often waited until heat had already started to bring the animals in.

"What about the cat? How's he doing?" Dr. Weiss stepped up to the cat's cage and looked in.

"Man! Is that cat ever a mess! Did it tangle with a tiger or something?"

"Looks like that, doesn't it?"

"Anyway, he seems to be doing fine. I took his temperature, and it's normal, but he's really torn up, isn't he?"

"It does look like he got the worst of it. Did you give it the antibiotic last night and this morning?"

"Yes, of course, Dr. Weiss."

"Thanks for everything, Sheila. If you documented everything you did, you can go home now."

"It's all written on their charts and in the computer. Bye, Dr. Weiss."

"Bye, now." Dr. Weiss was in the process of talking himself into computerized medical records. He wasn't there yet though. He wasn't even close. But it did make him feel more "modern" to have everything computerized, although he still kept everything the "old-fashioned" way, to be safe. That's what Carla always told him—that he was old-fashioned. Chuckling to himself, he returned to his office to sit at the computer and check out his appointments for the day. He could hear voices in the reception area, so clients were already filing into the building.

CHAPTER FOUR

WHEN Angelika turned ten years old in 1930, she disrupted the Schluter household with her angry cries and temper tantrums. She wanted to join the Young Girls League, a division of Hitler Youth, but her parents forbade it. It wasn't until she described to her parents how separate and different she felt—because all her friends were involved—that they relented and allowed her to join. They had looked at each other, horror-struck, and immediately signed her up. In the group, she enjoyed sports, hiking, singing, and weekend camping trips.

When she turned fourteen years old, she was promoted to the League of German Girls on April twentieth—Hitler's birthday—when all new members joined. Angelika gladly took the oath, "I promise always to do my duty in the Hitler Youth, in love and loyalty to the Führer" and then gave a crisp Nazi salute before joining her friends in celebration.

Angelika felt proud to wear her uniform of a full blue skirt, middy blouse, and heavy marching shoes. She felt like she belonged; she was part of something—something bigger than herself. And when they taught her about racial defilement and encouraged youth rallies where they marched against Jews, Gypsies, and any other non-Aryans, she embraced it with her whole heart and was one of the most ardent participants. A year passed with Angelika's hate of the Jews increasing.

The League of German Girls encouraged rebellion against parents, which came easily for Angelika, because she found her parents way too passive where the Führer was concerned. Her father had been *forced* to join the Nazi Party, and she had never seen either of them *initiate* a "Heil Hitler." She didn't like associating with them at all, and luckily, now that she was older, she didn't have to.

One evening after a successful rally, where they had broken some Jews' windows and sent others running for cover, fifteen-year-old Angelika Schluter barged through the front door with her Nazi armband blazing. When she saw her parents sitting quietly on the davenport, she raised her arm and shouted, "Heil Hitler" as a salute.

"Angelika," her father said quietly, "we need to talk to you."

"I know you disapprove of my Nazi activities, but I don't care! I can do what I want! You're just a bunch of Jew-lovers, anyway! You're lucky I don't turn you in!" Then she gave another quick salute and started walking briskly from the room before her mother called her back.

"Angelika, this is important."

She turned around and placed both hands on her hips. "Okay! What do you want then?"

"We *are* Jew-lovers, Angelika. We—"

"I knew it! I knew it!" Angelika interrupted and point-

16

ed at them.

"We love *you*, Angelika. And *you* are a Jew," her mother said quietly.

"Oh, that is so wrong! I can't believe you would lie to me just to get me to stop!" Angelika moved toward the door again, when her father spoke.

"We're not lying, Angelika. I swear to you."

Then her mother said, "Come here."

"Stop lying to me! That's not right! That's a terrible lie to tell someone! Especially me! I *hate* Jews!"

"Come here, Angelika," her mother whispered.

Angelika approached her mother warily. Her mother reached out and dropped the gold necklace into Angelika's hand.

She looked at both of them with absolute horror on her face. As soon as the gold star touched her hand she knew the truth about herself. "Oh my God," she mumbled, "oh my God, it's true. Oh my God, oh my God."

Angelika turned slowly with the star clasped tightly in her hand. Her father said, "You know what this means, don't you, Angelika? You're in danger. We've covered the tracks well, but nothing is for certain where the Nazis are concerned. You need to be careful and watch yourself."

She turned toward him, said, "Duh—" and walked down the hall toward her bedroom, still clasping the Jewish star in her hand.

To her parents' dismay, Angelika still wore the Nazi armband to school the next day and stayed for the usual League meeting. She came home early. The following day she left the armband at home, but stayed until the League meeting was over. Then she wore the armband to school, but skipped the meeting altogether. On the rare days she attended the rallies, she made sure she screamed the loudest so that everyone could see how zealous she still was.

It took more than a week before Franz and Gerta Schluter realized what their daughter was doing. Instead of stopping her Nazi activities immediately, which would have drawn attention to herself, she was weaning herself away from them a little at a time. After a while, no one would notice if she was there or not. A smart girl, that Angelika, a very smart girl.

CHAPTER FIVE

OVERNIGHT, Dean's attitude changed to reflect his parents' attitude. He didn't cancel plans for the move or even mention canceling the plans, but something subtle had shifted inside him. Angela could feel it. Instead of their usual lively conversations about how exciting their future would be, his half of the conversation was always dark and pessimistic. He called it *realistic*, but it seemed funny that "we can definitely find jobs" had suddenly changed to "maybe we can find jobs and maybe we can't."

It sounded pessimistic to Angela. She tried to maintain her excitement and enthusiasm for the move, but walking into the house with Dean frowning and stomping around, always brought her down. Although she tried to perk up Dean's spirits with talk of the new hikes they would take and how wonderful their life in New Hampshire would be, Dean continued moping around.

One day, after having had enough of his sulking, she put her hands on her hips and looked at him. "Do you

19

want to go or not, Dean? I'm tired of you looking like a kid who lost his teddy bear. What exactly is it that you want?"

He scowled and turned away. "I don't know what I want!"

Not wanting to leave the topic until it was resolved, she took several steps and stood in front of him again. "Dean, if you don't want to go, just say so, and we won't go. I hate it that you're so unhappy. Tell me what to do that would cheer you up."

"I don't know! We can't stay here! You know that! But what if we can't find jobs? We're spending all our savings just to move there. If we can't find jobs, how will we get back? It's like we can't stay and we can't go!"

Angela tried to remain calm. "All right, how about if we stay here, but you look for a job somewhere else? The grocery store pays really well. You could put in an application there. Or, if it would make you feel better, you can try to transfer for a different position where you are, like your parents suggested."

"No! I don't want to do that! I don't want to end up working a job that I hate in a place that I hate, like Dad had to do for all those years!"

Continuing in a slow, soothing voice, Angela said, "How about the grocery store? What's wrong with that idea? Then we can stay close to your parents." She didn't know why she said that. To calm him or to tick him off, but there it was.

"No! Let's just move! I'm not going to talk about it anymore!" Dean stormed out of the room.

He seemed better after that, but barely. Since he was still having chest pains despite the moving plans—or at that point, maybe *because* of them—he gave his notice and quit work several weeks before Angela. He did some packing, but mostly his own belongings or things that weren't fragile. Dean was responsible, but impatient. He was not careful enough to pack dishes or anything else breakable. So Angela ended up working all day and packing all night. It was a rough several weeks for Angela, and by the time the moving van pulled away from the curb and they had cleaned the house, Angela felt exhausted.

They took off in their overloaded car with Dean driving and Angela navigating. The trip east was uneventful except for some minor problems with their aging Rottweiler, Lady, and their mischievous cat, Velvet. Lady had several health problems including sore legs, which made it difficult for her to get in and out of the car for potty breaks. Velvet mostly behaved herself, but only because she wasn't allowed freedom inside the car. Since they were traveling in the heat of the summer, it was difficult to keep everyone hydrated.

Six days and three thousand miles later, their last day on the road involved driving thirteen hours through too many construction sites and too many small towns with twenty-five mile per hour speed limits. They arrived in Thoreau, New Hampshire, exhausted. They were both too tired and cranky to appreciate the beauty of the place and the differences from where they had just come. And although Angela's spirits rose and her mood lifted when they drove past the "Entering Thoreau, New Hampshire" sign, Dean continued to feel depressed. His chest pains may have disappeared since he quit work, but depression had replaced them. Angela wasn't sure which was worse. And then they drove up to the house that they had rented online and got a big surprise.

21

CHAPTER SIX

AFTER checking the appointments for the day, Dr. Weiss sat back in his chair, checked the clock above the doorway, and chuckled. Looking at the clock always made him chuckle. It was a dark-colored dog with green eyes wearing a white lab coat. The dog had a stethoscope around its neck, and its tail moved back and forth. Several years before, Carla and Curtis had given it to him as a gift. Every time Helen came into the office to see him—which was thankfully rare—she complained about how childish the clock was and that he should get rid of it. A lot she knew.

It was one of his favorite things, and he would get rid of her before he got rid of that clock! Not that he would, of course. He wasn't that kind of man—the divorcing kind. He had made a commitment, and he would honor it. No matter how miserable he was or how unfulfilling his marriage had become. It was a commitment. Period.

Megan interrupted his thoughts when she stuck her head through the door. "Dr. Weiss? You ready for the

22

first appointment?"

"Yes, Megan. Go ahead and bring them in."

The girl disappeared and a second later, he heard the announcement in the waiting room. Megan was a cute, little thing. With green eyes and a boy-cut of shaggy blonde hair, she was barely over five feet tall, but incredibly strong. She could hold a struggling Saint Bernhard or Mastiff with no problem. Dr. Weiss had no concerns when she was his tech. He stood up, straightened his tie, and prepared for his first patient. Then he picked up the chart by the door and briefly glanced at it.

Walking into the first examining room, Dr. Weiss shook the man's hand, nodded to the woman, and then knelt to check on the dog, a large German Shepherd. The man had run over the dog, broken its leg, and caused a large rip in its chest. "How are ya, boy?" Dr. Weiss petted the dog's head and smiled at him. Feeling the dog's chest, he looked up with angry eyes. "His chest is infected! Haven't you been cleaning it like I showed you? I was afraid this would happen!"

"We don't have time to clean his damn chest! Why can't he just lick it clean like the cat does?" The man smirked and puffed out his chest. He didn't need to look bigger, though, he towered over Dr. Weiss. His wife stood there, not saying a word.

Dr. Weiss stood up and gripped the edge of the examining table. He was afraid if his hand was loose that he might try to hit the man. Speaking slowly and enunciating every word, he said, "Because he can't reach it. It's under his chin. You said *you'd* take care of it, that the dog was important to you."

The man laughed but didn't make eye contact. "Not that important! Hey hey."

23

Dr. Weiss stuck his head out the door. "Megan!" Then, with his hand on the dog's head, he looked at the man. "I'll remove his cast and keep him for a few days to treat the infection."

The woman whispered something into the man's ear. The man cleared his throat. "We can't afford to put any more money into this dog!"

"It's included in the price I originally quoted you for the injury." Dr. Weiss knew if he sent the dog home with them and they didn't take care of it, the dog could die. He couldn't let that happen.

"Fine. We'll call you in a few days." Without another word, the man turned around and ushered his wife out the door.

Dr. Weiss closed his eyes and clenched his teeth. He knew he could find a good home for the dog. It wasn't papered that he knew of, but it was a big shepherd with a great personality. Those people didn't deserve a good dog like this. He hoped they never called back.

"Yes, Dr. Weiss." Megan stood in the doorway waiting for instruction.

"Put the next people in the examining room, and then take this guy in the back to x-ray his broken leg. After that, clean up that wound on his chest, and give him antibiotics." He wrote down the details and handed the slip of paper to her. "I'll be back there after examining the next dog—it's just a quick check—and you can help me take the cast off, if the x-ray shows that it's healed. It should be. Thanks."

Megan nodded, checked the list of appointments, and walked into the second examining room where she would put the next clients. Shaking his head, Dr. Weiss kneeled down to look at the wound again. He mumbled under his breath, then Megan walked back in to take the dog.

Dr. Weiss took a deep breath, looked at the chart, and strode into the next examining room. After giving the dog, a cute little Yorkie, a quick check, he told the woman that her dog was good to go. Then he walked to the back area to remove the shepherd's cast.

"Here it is, Dr. Weiss. It looks healed." Megan showed him the x-ray.

"Yes, looks fine. Let's do this." They removed the cast, and the dog was fine, not needing any sedation. He patted the dog on the head and looked at Megan. "After you clean his wound, put him in the kennel in the back. He'll be with us for a few days, until we can get that wound to heal. Those people would have killed him if I had let him go home with them."

The rest of the day flew by for Dr. Weiss, as it always did. He loved animals, and he loved his job. He didn't know what he'd do without it. When the last client left, he sat in his office reading over all the charts from the day. Not wanting to make any mistakes, he always re-checked the charts before he passed them on. Dr. Weiss set aside the shepherd's chart, since it would be with them, and put the rest of them in his out box. Kelsey would collect them and put them away first thing in the morning.

Putting his hand on the computer mouse, he clicked the internet browser to check his email. He wasn't a fan of computers, but after Carla called him old-fashioned, he thought he should at least have email. That was a few years ago, and it was fortunate. The results of some of the more complex tests that he sent out came in through email. After deleting the spam, he had no personal messages. Just as well, he thought.

Then he turned off the computer and sat on the easy chair on the other side of the office. Picking up the latest issue of *Journal of the American Veterinary Medical Association*, he began to read. After that, he had the new *Scientific American*. He glanced at the doggie-doctor clock and nodded. With any luck, it would take him a couple hours to get through the magazines, and then he would go check on the dogs that were staying over. He didn't have to go home for a long time. Thankfully.

CHAPTER SEVEN

AFTER completing the mandatory one year of land service—she could have chosen domestic work, but chose the farm—she returned to Munich to attend college, studying psychology. When she was twenty years old, Angelika married Dieter Richter, a young attorney she met while he was still in school. They lived together in a large house in the country not far from where she had been raised.

Two years later, she still attended the university hoping to become a psychiatrist following her idols, Jung, the Swiss psychotherapist, and Freud, the Austrian neurologist. Because of Freud's Jewish heritage, the university did not teach his ideas. Angelika, however, was able to get some black market books from one of her more radical professors, who said that although Freud was Jewish, some of his ideas had merit and were worth studying. Since her teacher suggested it, she didn't feel guilty having a forbidden Jewish book in the house, and she studied every word.

She came home one Sunday afternoon after visiting relatives for the weekend. Although she didn't see Dieter, she walked to the back of the house where she loved to gaze at the meadow, the flower garden, and the old trees. There, to her surprise, loped a large black German Shepherd dog.

Angelika turned as Dieter came into the room. "You got me a dog! I love you! I love you! Thank you for getting me a dog! I've wanted one so much! Thank you!"

She sprang from his arms and bolted for the door. He caught her and turned her around to face him. She looked at him puzzled.

"He's not your dog, Angelika. He's my brother's dog."

"Your brother? I didn't even know you had a brother!"

Dieter sighed. "He's my step-brother, actually. I didn't want to tell you about him." He looked down, not wanting to see her eyes. "I was afraid you wouldn't marry me if you knew about him."

Angelika laughed and broke out of his grasp. She pushed her hands against his chest. "I would still marry you! I would always marry you! Why would I care if you have a brother? Is he cuter than you?" she teased.

"Angelika," he said seriously, "my brother is an officer in the German army. He's a Nazi—I mean, a real Nazi." Angelika knew Dieter alluded to the fact that he, also, was a member of the Nazi Party. Anyone who wasn't a member was suspect and risked all manner of trouble with the authorities.

Angelika narrowed her vision and stepped back from him. "Have you told him—?" she asked nervously.

"No, of course not. Believe me, I know the consequences." Dieter referred to the abduction of Jews all over Germany and the rumors of the death camps. And his brother was part of it. With a soft voice and still not making eye contact, Dieter explained how it was too terrible for him to even think about—especially since he had a Jewish wife whom he loved dearly. "You understand, then? Why I didn't tell you?"

Angelika nodded. "But why would your brother be a Nazi? You grew up in the same family. How could you be so different?"

"We didn't grow up in the same family. He had a different father who died when Rolf was a teenager. My mother remarried. Rolf had already gone off to school when I was five. I barely know him."

"But a Nazi— Well, I still like his dog! Can I bring him in the house?"

"Rolf said to leave him alone in the yard. He doesn't know you—or me, really—and he could be dangerous."

"Nah, dogs love me!"

"All the same, Angelika, I would feel better if you left the dog alone."

Disappointed, Angelika's head slumped momentarily. "Well, what's his name? You can tell me his name, can't you?"

Dieter grabbed her and kissed her. "I missed you! Yes, I can tell you his name! It's Beowulf, and Rolf calls him Wulfie." Then the phone rang, and Dieter left her alone by the window.

Angelika watched him go and then she turned, quickly walked to the door, and slipped outside, grabbing something out of her purse as she went. She knelt down, clapped her hands, and called to the dog. "Wulfie! Wulfie!"

The dog turned and looked at her, and for a moment, she could feel the fear rising in her belly. But she pushed it down and smiled at the dog while holding out the tasty morsel of sausage left over from her travels. Beowulf smelled the sausage and bounded toward her taking it gently out of her hand. Then the dog let her stroke him and hug him. In a few minutes, he lay on his back while she tickled his stomach.

When Dieter opened the door, Beowulf jumped up on guard. When he saw it was Dieter, he relaxed back into Angelika's petting. "I should have known better than to leave you alone with him! You are a charmer! I guess I had nothing to worry about!" Dieter walked over and looked down at the two of them.

Angelika smiled up at him and continued stroking the large dog. "It's okay. You can pet him too." By the time she dragged herself to bed that evening, she had spent several hours playing with and petting Wulfie.

Later that night, just before Angelika fell into a peaceful sleep, she heard Dieter's and a stranger's voices downstairs. She had enjoyed Beowulf and would miss him.

CHAPTER EIGHT

THE moving truck, which wasn't expected for several more days, had beaten them to their new rented house. The house was at the base of a steep hill, and the truck was parked at an angle. When Dean and Angela arrived, the movers had already unloaded most of the furniture and boxes. They wouldn't have to sleep on the floor after all—a welcome surprise after a hard day of driving.

It was the first they'd seen of the house, except for the pictures on the internet. It was an old farmhouse, needed paint, but not badly, with big windows, and a big tree in the front yard. Maybe not exactly what they expected, not idyllic as they hoped, but it was home, and it was far away from the stress and chaos of their earlier lives.

The following day, they started unpacking. Angela had brought everything she thought they might ever need. There were a ton of boxes to unpack. The first full day in Thoreau, they did more resting than unpacking, but the house was coming together. Dean wanted to just unpack unpack unpack until they finished, but Angela wanted to leave the house and check out Thoreau. It had been more than nine years since they were there, and much had changed.

"We need to unpack! This house is a mess!" Dean didn't look up from his unpacking.

"We can come back to it later. It will wait."

"I can't live like this! We need to unpack!"

He walked out of the room putting something away. Angela followed. "Dean, you sat on your butt for a month while I worked. *I* need a break!" She walked out without waiting for his response and slammed the door behind her. She drove to a nearby lake, sat on the soft ground, and listened to the water lap the edges of the shore and the wind blowing through the trees. And she relaxed and thought about what was going on between her and Dean.

The pall—over their relationship and their lives—had followed them to Thoreau, and Angela didn't like that at all. Before the chest pains from his job started, she and Dean had rarely argued. Until their most recent turbulent times, they had gotten along really well. But the chest pains, the move, and now the arrival in Thoreau had turned them into a squabbling couple. It was ugly. And it was not something that Angela was used to; and she had no intention of getting used to it.

As she breathed in the cool lake air, she wondered if she had made a mistake moving Dean out here across the country away from his family. She wondered if she should have left him before they ever made their move. It would have been easier on her that way. And Dean? She could have left him to deal with the chest pains on his own. But would he, or would he have just let the stress kill him? No, she couldn't have left him in those circumstances to deal with it on his own. There was still love there—at least she thought there might be—and she cared what happened to him. Dean was a smart guy, but he was too stressed to even try to figure out what to do for himself.

But now what? He was still being grumpy and unco-operative and stressed out when there was nothing to feel stressed about. Then she remembered the fears of his family—that they might not find jobs and that Dean might kill himself because of it. What a thing to even suggest to him! Nodding her head to herself, she admitted that maybe there *was* something to feel stressed about. Finding a job.

Angela sighed and remembered back to after they had decided to leave but before they had left. She had done enough internet searching to know where she wanted to apply for a job. So she visualized herself working for Thoreau Internet Service, saw in her mind's eye wearing one of their t-shirts and walking out of the building that was on their website.

Dean would do no such thing. It didn't help that he had no idea what he wanted to do. But again, he wouldn't help himself either. Even all those weeks on the couch waiting for her to quit work, he spent no time considering what he might want to do, no time investi-gating places that he might want to apply for work. Granted, he wasn't that fluent with computers, but they were still receiving the local Thoreau paper, and she didn't think he had ever even picked it up to look at the help wanted ads. She couldn't leave him, but at the same time, how could she stay?

CHAPTER NINE

THE dog doctor clock above the door ticked to nine o'clock, and Dr. Weiss forced himself to stand. After one more quick check to the animals in the back, he locked up and drove home. Curtis was under the lights in the driveway playing basketball with two of his friends. Dr. Weiss strode past, waved, and continued to the front door of the house. Sighing, he stood there a moment, closed his eyes briefly and opened the door.

The television wasn't on. What a relief! Helen was already upstairs in the bedroom, so he wouldn't have to deal with her. He didn't want to get into yet another yelling match. Why did they do that, anyway? They never used to argue. Why had their relationship deteriorated so far that they couldn't spend five minutes together without an argument? What a way to live. Then he reminded himself once again that he had made a commitment, a vow, and he was not the kind of man to break that, no matter what.

Wolf sprinted out of the kitchen and skidded to a stop

in front of him. "Wolf!" he said quietly. "That's my boy!" Dr. Weiss knelt down to pet the dog and put his face into the big dog's scruff.

Then he stood up and, followed by the big dog, shuffled into the kitchen, opened the refrigerator, and pulled out the dinner that Helen had put away for him. When was the last time they had eaten dinner together? He couldn't even remember. Pulling off the aluminum foil, he looked at the food and nodded. Lean roast beef and asparagus. She was a good cook, he'd give her that. Shoving the plate into the microwave, he returned to the refrigerator, pulled out his salad, and sat down at the table to eat. His place was already set at the head of the table—as if it mattered. He always ate alone! Not that he was complaining; he preferred that rather than stare at her from across the table, neither of them with anything to say to the other that didn't include yelling.

Looking down at the dog, settled in by his feet, he smiled. "I'm not alone when I'm with you, Wolf!"

When Dr. Weiss was halfway through his meal, his son popped through the kitchen door bouncing his basketball through the room. "Oh, sorry, Dad!" Curtis held the basketball in his hands as he walked by his father, and continued bouncing when he left the room.

Dr. Weiss shook his head, laughed to himself, and continued eating. Teenagers! Curtis was a good kid, and Dr. Weiss knew that. Both his kids were, but Carla, he nodded, yeah, Carla was his favorite. She had been from the moment of her birth. He loved Curtis—a lot—but he supposed there was something special about fathers and daughters. He and Carla were especially close. Not as close as they were before she became a rebellious teenager, but still, close.

As if on cue, Carla came through the door, talking on her iPhone. When she saw her dad sitting at the table, she ended her conversation and slid the phone into her pocket. "Hi, Daddy."

"Hi, sweetheart. How was your day?"

She stood behind the chair next to him with her hands on top of it. "Fine. Same-o, same-o, you know?"

He nodded.

"And yours? How was your day, Daddy?"

He looked at her with a broad grin across his face. "Like being in heaven itself. I *love* my job."

"Only it's not a job to you, is it Dad? It's your whole life!"

"Yes, Carla, I suppose it is. There's still room for you in it though!"

She laughed and walked to the doorway. "Is Mom upstairs again?"

"Yeah, I think so."

She frowned. "Sorry you have to eat alone, Dad. I'd stay with you longer, but I have to go study."

"Thanks, Carla. I appreciate any time you can give me. You know that."

Carla turned back into the room, came up behind him, and kissed him on the top of his head. Then she walked away while pulling her iPhone out of her pocket.

Dr. Weiss watched her go and wondered why she had frowned like that. Did she think it was his fault that her mother spent so much time upstairs instead of with him? But she had to have heard the arguments and yelling matches. She was old enough to know that things were not right between them. Did she blame him for that? *Was* he to blame? How do you even know in a situation like this, he wondered. Maybe it *was* his fault. If it was, it wasn't deliberate. He was certain of that. He shook his head and hoped that he wouldn't let Carla down by contributing to the disintegration of his marriage.

CHAPTER TEN

GERMANY 1940

ANGELIKA loved her garden and loved working in it. She loved it so much and found so much peace there. It was away from not only the university, but also everything else that was going on in the city—the things she had once been a part of. But everything was different now, and she had her garden to amuse her.

Although she had wanted to plant vegetables, Dieter was against it. He said if the neighbors found out she was planting vegetables, then they might think that he didn't have enough money to support her. It was bad enough, he had said, that she's attending school for a *career* instead of staying home, keeping house, and having babies as was promoted for women all over Germany. She had scoffed at his deprecation of her career, but bowed to his wishes to not plant vegetables. Now her flower garden was a spectacle to be seen.

The yard was awash with colors of red, blue, pink, purple, yellow, and white. Angelika cultivated roses, lilies, carnations, sunflowers, and others. And there were also other plants in the yard besides flowers, including bamboo and several varieties of ferns. She remembered when she had looked out the window and seen Beowulf there. It was funny, but as much as she loved her garden, she didn't wonder for a second if the dog would spoil any of her carefully tended flowers. The longing for a dog of her own overshadowed any concern about the flowers. As it turned out, he did nothing to hurt the flowers. Thinking back, she thought maybe he was just glad to be outside and running free—free, at least within the confines of their large yard.

It was when she was outside tending to her garden and thinking about Beowulf—whom she had only seen that one time several weeks before—that she heard voices inside the house and came inside to investigate. In the hall stood a tall man in a Nazi officer's uniform. Sitting obediently by his side was Beowulf. Angelika ran toward the dog with arms outstretched. Her eyes were focused on the dog, and she didn't see how the man stiffened with panic until he shouted, "Stop! The dog will hurt you! Stop right there!"

Angelika didn't stop. She had no intention of stopping. Before she reached the dog, whose tail was wagging at the sight of her, he had bounded toward her. When they met, she threw her arms around his neck giving him a big hug. She kneeled down and Beowulf rolled over for Angelika to scratch his tummy.

"Ah, my little brother has found himself a beautiful wife. But she doesn't listen very well, does she—?"

"Angelika," Dieter said, "this is my brother, Rolf. Captain Rolf." Dieter hesitated and continued. "And Rolf, this is my wife, Angelika."

"My pleasure, Angelika." Rolf made an exaggerated

bow. "I've never seen Wulfie act like that with anyone but me. He's trained to kill," he said casually, like every other dog on the block was trained to kill.

"All dogs like me. It's been like that my whole life. But I've met Wulfie before. Last time you left him here."

"Hmmmm," Rolf said as he walked closer. He stood above the girl and the dog looking down at them.

Angelika looked up at Rolf, exposing the fleshy area of her throat to the dog. She noticed Rolf's concern until he saw Wulfie raise his head and lick her smooth neck.

"Why is the dog trained to kill?" she asked.

"Because that's his job!" Rolf answered harshly before clicking his heels and turning to his brother. "So, Dieter, is it all right if I stay here for an occasional weekend? The drive back to Berlin has grown very tiresome."

"Yes, Rolf, I don't see a problem with that."

Rolf called the dog to him by clapping his hands together once, and then he turned toward the open front door. Angelika watched as Wulfie followed Rolf. Then she got up and stood beside Dieter. "Captain Rolf?" she said as he approached the doorway. Rolf turned and raised his eyebrows in question. "Will you bring Wulfie with you when you come back?"

"Wulfie never leaves my side!" Rolf said and strode out the door.

"He did today," Angelika said loud enough for him to hear.

She saw Rolf's shoulders move with a quick chuckle at her comment, but he kept walking toward his car, Wulfie by his side.

CHAPTER ELEVEN

PRESENT DAY

DEAN and Angela had arrived in Thoreau on a Wednesday, their tenth wedding anniversary. On the following Monday, Angela was ready to look for a job—at Thoreau Internet Service where she had been visualizing her employment. When she drove up, she saw that it was a brick building that used to be a bank. The drive-up windows no longer functioned, but the clock on the pole by the street did. It said eight-fifty-five when she arrived, and her interview was at nine. Perfect timing, she thought.

When Angela walked in, Sharleen, the personnel manager, greeted her. They shook hands, and then Sharleen led Angela into her office. They sat on either side of Sharleen's desk, which faced the large window. Sharleen picked up Angela's resumé, which she had sent even before they moved.

"How long were you at Hooper International?" Sharleen looked at her with a smile.

"Seven years, but my first two years were in the payroll

department. Then they had an opening in the computer department, and I got the job because of my prior experience." Angela, feeling confident, smiled.

"Yes, I see that." After several more questions, Sharleen said, "We could use someone like you, but we won't have anything available for three weeks. Do you think you could start then?"

"Absolutely!"

Sharleen stood up to end the interview. "All right, Angela. I can't make any promises, but I'll call you when something opens up."

"That's great, Sharleen. Thank you."

Angela walked out of the internet building and felt fantastic. She knew she had the job. There was no doubt in her mind. She had visualized it. She had created it. But being an overachiever, she still applied for other jobs while she waited to hear from Sharleen.

Dean checked the newspaper every day, but since it was a small newspaper, he could go through the want-ads in five minutes. He saw nothing that appealed to him, so he stayed home and watched television. His negative attitude, which began with his parents' comments before they moved, worsened. He became moody and uncommunicative. To say that he was not much fun to be around was like saying that a rabid dog running toward you with tongue lolling and jaws snapping was kind of worrisome. He was miserable, and it made Angela miserable.

When she considered everything, she knew Dean wasn't a slug. If she thought of herself as a type A overachieving personality, then Dean was a triple A plus plus plus overachieving personality. That's what was so confusing. His chest pains had vanished, but so had all of his motivation. It depressed her to watch him, to be around him, or even just to talk to him. And she didn't know what to do for him besides give him encouraging comments and point out jobs that sounded interesting. She felt helpless.

Two weeks later, Thoreau Internet Service called and hired Angela for tech support. She drove to work every day and came home to Dean watching television. He sent out a few resumés, but they lacked energy and enthusiasm and drew no responses.

Although it felt like forever to Angela, it was only a few weeks later that Dean finally accepted a job as a filing clerk. It was only part time, with the promise of full time "soon" and a possibility of advancement. Here he was starting at the bottom again. Both of them felt the smack of that. His college degree had hurt more than helped in the caliber of jobs that were available in the small town. He was so overqualified that most places refused to even interview him. They both knew that it was luck that got him the filing job.

Dean didn't mind the job too much and enjoyed the people he worked with. He worked three days a week, and although it wasn't much, at least it was something. Angela noticed that he wasn't as depressed on the days that he worked. But mostly, he still clung to his negative attitude, and it touched everything he did.

The two of them together still weren't making enough money to think about buying a house and that bothered both of them. One reason they had decided on Thoreau was that houses were in their price range. Now they found that their price range wasn't their price range any more because of how little money they made.

Life went on. Velvet enjoyed the windows in the old

farm house and would sit in one or the other of them and preen herself through the day. Lady enjoyed running through the field behind their house. Sometimes she was crazy, though, and ran straight through the brambles without bowing her head to avoid them. What happened next was no surprise.

CHAPTER TWELVE

THE morning dawned, and Dr. Weiss jumped out of bed—carefully, though, so as not to wake Helen. But something bothered him. He moved his shoulders trying to stop the feeling. It didn't work. What was bothering him anyway?

Walking into the bathroom, he suddenly remembered. It was Carla. The way she had looked at him last night. Frowning. After his shave and shower, he walked downstairs to drink the coffee that Curtis had once again fixed for him. He sat at the table still thinking about Carla. She may be a teenager, but it was obviously still important to her that her parents stay together. He couldn't let her down, and he knew that he'd have to make more of an effort to rejuvenate his and Helen's flagging marriage.

When he finished his coffee, he walked to the other room for a pen and paper and wrote a note to Helen, which he left on the kitchen table where she was sure to see it. *Dear Helen, I would love to take you out to dinner tonight. A real date! We haven't done that for years. How about it? It will*

45

be fun! Just like old times! Please say yes. Love, Ralph. He read it over several times, decided that it said exactly what he wanted to say, and left for work.

As he was about to leave, Wolf bounced through the dog door and pushed against his legs. "It's about time you come in to say good morning to me, Wolf! Bye, now!" He stroked the dog and walked out the door.

Dr. Weiss smiled all the way to work. He felt he was doing something positive, and that it would make Carla feel better about him. And who knows? Maybe he and Helen would have fun. Maybe they'd enjoy each other, just like old times. Thinking about which restaurant to choose, he decided on an expensive one with dim lighting and candles. The place they'd gone to the night he had asked her to marry him! Perfect! Helen would like that.

They'd have a good evening and a romantic night. Dr. Weiss couldn't remember the last time they'd had a romantic night. That part of their lives had just slipped away, slowly at first, and then it was gone. They hadn't been romantic in several years. It was time to make a positive change in his marriage, and this was it. Dinner, dancing, yes, it would be perfect. When he arrived at the clinic, he immediately called their downstairs phone, which he knew wouldn't wake her. And he left a message about the restaurant and the dancing. She would be so pleased. It would be a wonderful evening and would turn their lives—and their love—around. It would make everything better.

He was always happy at work—it was the only place he *was* happy—but today, he had an extra spring to his step. When his clients started coming in, he was so focused that he had forgotten about his plans. When he

46

had a cancellation and a quick break at ten-thirty that morning, he found a voicemail from Helen waiting for him. Excited, he dialed the number and could hardly wait to hear her voice. But it wasn't what he expected. She said it sounded like a nice idea, but he should have given her more notice. She had already defrosted a chicken and planned to cook it this evening. He was welcome to join her when she ate at six o'clock, and maybe they could go to the restaurant next week or the week after that.

Dr. Weiss plopped the phone down on the desk. Disappointed wasn't the word for what he was feeling. He felt like an abject failure. He should have checked the refrigerator. Wait, why couldn't the chicken wait another day? Grabbing the phone, he started tapping her number, and then put down the phone. Her voice. Her voice wasn't excited about his offer at all. It sounded tired and disdainful—just like she always sounded. His shoulders slumped, and he sighed. Now what?

No. He wouldn't give up this easily. It was still a good idea, and he could still make it work. After work, he would stop and buy flowers and candy—Helen loved dark chocolates—and then bring them home to her. Maybe after her chicken dinner, he could put soft music on in the living room, and they could dance there. She used to love dancing to Sinatra—he never understood why—so he'd buy her a new Sinatra CD too. Excited, he moved on to his next client.

At three o'clock, in the middle of a poodle's emergency C-section and with his scheduled clients backing up, Dr. Weiss called out to a tech who was walking by. "Amanda, can you please tell Kelsey to call my wife and tell her that I won't be able to be home until 6:30 and to please hold dinner for me?"

"Sure thing, Dr. Weiss." Amanda strode past on her way to the front. A minute later, she returned. "I told her, and she'll do it right now."

As Amanda started walking away, Dr. Weiss called her back. "I need something else, Amanda. Are you too busy right now? I could really use a favor. Would you mind going to a florist and get a dozen red roses—in a nice vase—and then going to the store and get some expensive dark chocolates and a Sinatra CD?"

"Sinatra?"

Dr. Weiss nodded as he began sewing up the poodle. "Yes, I know. Helen loves him. Go figure."

"Sure, Dr. Weiss. I don't mind. I'll go right now."

"My credit card is in the top drawer of my desk. Thanks so much, Amanda!"

Two and a half hours later, Dr. Weiss had only one client to go: an examination and vaccinations. Kelsey had rescheduled several of the clients for later in the week, so he wasn't that behind after all. When he finished the last client, he walked into his office for the first time since after the C-section. A beautiful vase of red roses sat on his desk, along with a large box of dark chocolates and a Sinatra CD. Perfect.

After he finished updating the medical charts of the day, he gathered up the gifts in his arms and carried them out the door. He pulled up to the house at six twenty-five. He even got home on time. Everything was working out perfectly. Opening the kitchen door with a big smile on his face, he saw that Helen was almost finished eating. The shock of it made him stumble, but he didn't drop anything, and he refused to let it darken his mood.

"Helen! I brought you something!" He placed the roses, chocolates, and CD on the table in front of her.

"What's this for? Are you fooling around and feeling guilty or something?" She picked up the Sinatra CD. "And I have this one already." She tossed it back on the table, and it slid off onto the seat on the other side.

"I'm not feeling guilty about anything." He sank into the chair beside her, starting to feel deflated. "I thought we could, you know, start over. But you started dinner without me."

"You're late!" she said without looking at him.

"No, no. I had Kelsey call to say I'd be here at 6:30 and for you to wait."

"Do you know how many times I held dinner for you and ended up eating a cold meal? No more, Ralph."

He stood up. "All right. I know there have been times that I've done that. I'm sorry." When she said nothing, he picked up a plate, walked to the stove, and put his dinner on it. Chicken and rice casserole. He sat back down next to her. Shrugging his shoulders, he looked at her and smiled. "After dinner, would you like to dance?"

"Dance? With *you*? Are you kidding me?" She looked at him with fire in her eyes then pushed away from the table so hard that her chair almost fell over backward. Grabbing her plate off the table, she threw it into the sink where it shattered. "No way!" She scowled and then tromped past him out of the room.

CHAPTER THIRTEEN

GERMANY 1940

ROLF and Beowulf arrived late Friday evening after Angelika had gone to sleep. When she awoke Saturday morning, Wulfie met her at her bedroom door. She leaned down and wrapped her arms around the furry neck and hugged him. "You're beautiful," she whispered into his soft fur.

Walking downstairs with the dog at her side, Angelika smelled the aroma of eggs and bacon. She walked into the kitchen and saw Dieter at the stove cooking and Rolf sitting at the table.

"Ah, here's my beautiful boy now," Rolf said. "Come here, boy!"

"You better watch out, Rolf, I think Angelika has already stolen Wulfie's heart. She may just take him right away from you!" Dieter turned back to the eggs and flipped them over.

"Yeah, right," Rolf said scornfully. "The dog is trained to give his life for me, to kill for me. I don't think he will be so quick to desert me."

"Don't be so cynical, Captain Rolf! Wulfie met me by my door and left you all alone down here!" Angelika laughed. "He's already mine! You just haven't realized it yet!"

"Yes, but—" Rolf started.

"Children, children!" Dieter interrupted. "Let's stop this arguing and eat breakfast!" He set a plate in front of Rolf and one in front of Angelika.

"It smells great, brother! When did you learn to cook so well?" Rolf picked up his fork.

"I'm afraid that's my fault," said Angelika. "Cooking is not in my repertoire."

"Pray tell, what is in your repertoire then?" Rolf asked with a touch of sarcasm.

"She's studying to be a psychotherapist," Dieter said with finality. "Now can we eat in peace?" He set a plate on the table for himself, sat down, and began to eat.

Later that afternoon as Dieter worked in the garden and talked to Rolf, Angelika played with Wulfie by the stream. When the dog lay down with exhaustion, Angelika withdrew into the house.

She sat reading in the living room when Rolf came in and sat across from her. "What are you reading?" he asked.

"Just a textbook from school," she replied and kept reading.

"So you're going to be a psychotherapist, hmmm? Freudian, I presume?"

"Freudian! Why would you think that?" she asked, trying not to show her alarm.

"Because Freud's theories are the definitive theories for psychoanalysis."

"Freud's a Jew!" blurted Angelika.

51

"So what? That doesn't make his theories any less correct," Rolf said almost angrily.

"But you're a Nazi!" said Angelika.

"Aren't we all?" Rolf motioned around the room. "Besides, I may be a Nazi, but I'm still a thinking man."

"How could you be a Nazi and a thinking man? Those two don't go together," Angelika taunted.

Rolf looked at her and was about to answer when Angelika said, "You're a hypocrite! That's what you are, a hypocrite!"

"Respecting genius does not make me a hypocrite. Freud obviously has overcome the limitations of his race."

"Overcome his limitations, huh? Well, what would happen if he showed up in one of your so-called Concentration Camps? I've heard rumors that they are really death camps! Would you put him to death as easily as you kill the others?" she demanded.

"It is not my job to put anybody to death," he said slowly.

"No, you just train killer dogs, right? You're a captain in the Nazi army which means that you condone it."

Before Rolf could answer, Dieter charged in and said, "Children! Children! Do I have to put you in separate rooms? Every time you're in the same room you argue!"

Rolf stood up and took two steps toward Angelika who was now also standing. He reached out and put his hand on her arm. "You have spunk, young Angelika. I respect that."

She looked up at him and said, "And you're a thinking man. I respect that—in a Nazi."

Rolf smiled, clicked his heels, and strode out of the room, with Beowulf at his side. Dieter said to Angelika,

"He likes you."

"I like him, too," she shrugged. Then she looked at Dieter fearfully and whispered, "He doesn't know, does he?"

"No, my darling Angelika, he doesn't know, and he will not know. Your secret is safe with me." He hugged her close to him and kissed her softly on the forehead.

CHAPTER FOURTEEN

Running through the brambles had hurt Lady. She had something in her eye—something harmful. It was small and white and had started at the corner of her eye. Angela kept hoping it would go away, but instead it creeped its way across Lady's eye, growing in size as it advanced. Angela's excuse was that it would somehow go away by itself, but really, she didn't want to take her to the vet because she was more concerned about the money. The move had cost them much more than they had expected, and with Dean not working for so long, their savings had been depleted. It was a bad mistake to make, especially with Lady's tenuous health.

When the white spot wasn't going away but was only getting worse, Dean and Angela finally took Lady to a holistic veterinarian in another town. The vet acted distracted the entire time they were there and then wouldn't return Angela's calls. When the medicine given to Lady didn't fix the white spot, they decided to try another vet.

The next vet was a kind, older gentleman who gave Lady an eye ointment and said that if it didn't work, they should go to a specialist named Dr. Weiss in Berlin, New Hampshire. After ten days and no improvement, Angela made an appointment with Dr. Weiss. She didn't realize how much that little white spot would affect the rest of her life.

The drive to Dr. Weiss's clinic in Berlin was long but pretty. Besides the few small towns they passed, tall pine trees lined most of the way with an occasional farm replete with cows and horses grazing in lush, green pastures. One time, Angela thought she had seen a moose behind some of the trees, but Dean said it was just wishful thinking, which made her laugh.

The animal hospital was a large building surrounded by a large landscaped yard and a large nearly full parking lot on the south side. As they walked in to the building, they saw a picture of the owner, Dr. Weiss, along with his degrees. He was an attractive man in his mid-thirties.

The crowded waiting room had two cages of birds hanging from the ceiling and a loose cat that walked around on the counters. It was a homey place, and Angela immediately felt at ease there.

It wasn't long before they were called into an examining room. While they waited for the doctor to join them, Angela noticed how sterile everything seemed. The place impressed her. When Dr. Weiss walked into the room, he had an air of competence about him—or arrogance— she wasn't sure which. He shook both Dean's and Angela's hands with a firm grip and then looked at Lady's eye while Angela explained what had happened.

"Eye injuries need to be taken care of immediately," Dr. Weiss said gruffly. "It's really bad to wait like this on an eye injury."

Angela felt so guilty that she didn't even mention they had already been to two other veterinarians. She wasn't sure it would have mattered because she knew they had waited way too long regardless.

Dean and Angela both listened as Dr. Weiss talked about what he could do and what alternatives there were. Then Angela remembered Lady's history and knew she should mention it. Any treatment options needed to be reflective of Lady's past health conditions.

"Dr. Weiss, before Lady was two years old she had hemolytic anemia and almost died." She gave him the details of Lady's past condition and how it currently affected her. Something shifted in his eyes when Angela mentioned the hemolytic anemia though. It was as if he had previously put her and Dean in the category of neglectful pet owners who are unaware and possibly uneducated. Now, Angela's detailed knowledge of hemolytic anemia put her in a different category that he respected. Angela thought it was an interesting shift inside a fifteen-minute appointment.

They spoke briefly about what had happened, and Angela filled him in on Lady's transfusion and her week in intensive care. She wanted to be sure to erase the image of her and Dean as irresponsible pet owners. Dr. Weiss listened intently and then described the surgery that he recommended. He said it might restore most of Lady's sight. They had to do it, Angela thought. They might have been neglectful up until then, but now they needed to follow through and do the right thing for Lady. She was their baby, and she deserved the best. Dr. Weiss specialized in this kind of surgery. Angela and Dean trusted Dr. Weiss, so they made the appointment to bring her back for surgery on the following Tuesday.

CHAPTER FIFTEEN

DR. Weiss didn't have much time to think for the rest of the day. His clients were continuous until 6:30 when the last one left. It was okay though. He liked it that way. And when you love what you do, being busy like that is a bonus. But as he leisurely perused the medical charts for the day, he stopped when he picked up Lady the Rottweiler's chart.

That woman! She was something else. She was not only pretty with her long, dark hair and dark eyes, but she knew about hemolytic anemia! And she could talk about it intelligently like she knew exactly what she was talking about! He had to admit to himself that she impressed him. Then he remembered the man she was with and the ring on her finger. It didn't bother him though. It relieved him in a way. Not that he would ever be unfaithful to Helen—no matter what, he wouldn't be unfaithful to her—but still, he didn't need the temptation. That would be too frustrating. But he could think about her, dream about her, fantasize about her. Although he didn't

58

even know her name, it didn't matter. He didn't need to know, so with his hand, he covered the top part of the chart—where her name was—and continued his perusal. Dr. Weiss looked up, smiled at nothing in particular, and returned to checking out the rest of the charts.

When he finished, he gathered them together and with a new spring to his step, he walked them out to the reception room and dropped them into the *To Be Filed* box. He stood there and breathed in the peacefulness of the place. It was completely different after hours from the hectic pace of the day. Dr. Weiss enjoyed them both. The office cat, Sweetie Pie, jumped up onto the counter and meowed at him. Turning around, he petted the cat as she rubbed up against him, purring loudly. He leaned down, kissed her on the top of the head, and moved across the room to the two cages of parakeets.

"Hello, little ones." He stood in front of the cage with the new yellow parakeet. The dark blue one came to him, but the yellow one lingered back, took one nervous step forward, and then scurried to the other end of the cage. "It's okay, we'll get there. No rush." Speaking softly, with his finger to the cage where the blue parakeet was, he slowly moved his body to the other side. When he was halfway there, the yellow bird showed signs of fear, so he stopped and didn't continue until it settled. A minute later he stood in front of the bird, and it looked at him nervously, but didn't move, so he moved slowly away. After he had distanced himself from the bird, he said softly, "That's it. We'll go slow until you get to know me. I won't hurt you. I promise. We'll be friends." Smiling again, he walked back into his office, grabbed his magazines, and sank into his easy chair to read.

A few minutes later, after glancing at an article called

Keeping a Sterile Environment in Your Clinic—which he skipped because his clinic was always immaculate—the woman with the Rottweiler popped into his thoughts again, bringing another smile to his face. He luxuriated in the feeling and the thought of her until a heavy weight settled on his shoulders sucking every bit of joy out of him. Trying to shake it off, he was unsuccessful. What was it, he wondered.

Then he knew. The other night with Helen. He couldn't believe how horribly it had turned out. It wasn't just bad, it was a disaster! The only bright side of it was that relations with his wife were so bad they couldn't get any worse. His efforts to make them better had failed, and that made him feel bad. Was he the one who had destroyed their marriage? It didn't matter. Placing the blame on anyone—himself or her—wasn't doing anyone any good. Would he try that again—bringing her gifts and asking her out to a good dinner? No, they were too far gone for that. What else could he do? He'd have to think about that one. He owed it to her—and himself—to come up with something. There was no way he could leave her, but how could they possibly go on the way they were now?

CHAPTER SIXTEEN

ANGELIKA sat on the davenport studying when Beowulf jumped up beside her and kept licking her face. "Enough already, enough," she laughed as she pushed the big dog away.

"I have never seen my dog act that way with anyone else," Rolf said as he walked over to pull the dog away.

Angelika hugged and kissed the big dog. "It's all right. We love each other." Beowulf rolled over and let Angelika rub his stomach. As she scratched, his tail wagged and one of his hind legs moved in the air. She and Rolf both laughed.

Rolf sat at the other end of the davenport shaking his head. "It's like he has known you forever!"

"I must have known him in a former lifetime!" joked Angelika.

Rolf looked at her thoughtfully. "So why do you prefer Jung over Freud?" he asked.

"The collective unconscious. I love the idea that we are all connected, all one. It makes me feel like I'm part

61

of something greater than myself—something important." Rolf nodded his head without saying anything.

"And synchronicities," continued Angelika, "meaningful coincidences. I love those, and the more I acknowledge the ones I have, the more I have them. It's like they are confirming my place in the universe. I just think it's a great way to look at life—that there is more out there than what we see." She adjusted the dog's head in her lap and then continued. "When I read Freud, I get the feeling that he thinks there is less out there—that it is all in our heads. That just doesn't resonate with me!"

Rolf nodded his understanding. "I understand what you're saying, but I would argue that coincidences are coincidences and that it is the power of our own minds that gives them meaning. For instance, if you never knew what a German Shepherd dog was, when you saw one it wouldn't register. Once you knew what one looks like, however, you would see them all the time. Does that mean there are suddenly more German Shepherds in the world or that the sight of one means something? I don't think so." He shook his head. "You are just more aware, more knowledgeable than you were before."

"I really disagree," said Angelika. "There are no coincidences."

Rolf smiled. "All right then, give me an example of one of your synchronicities."

"All right." Angelika's eyes sparkled at him. "I had only been at the university for a few months, and I was feeling lonely and a little depressed. I started thinking of my graduation night and what a good time I had dancing with my boyfriend. At that moment, another student came around a corner singing the song that Gunther and

I referred to as our song! It made me feel better just hearing it. That's synchronicity!"

"And I would say that your ears probably heard the melody before your mind could assimilate it and that made you think of young Gunther," Rolf said and shrugged.

"Okay, how about this one? What if on my way home I had been thinking of how much I wanted a dog, and then I got home and Beowulf was here? How about that!"

"That didn't happen, though, did it?" asked Rolf. "Besides, Wulfie isn't your dog, he's mine."

Angelika leaned forward and snuggled into Wulfie's warm fur. The dog lifted his head and licked her again. "So you say—" smiled Angelika.

"All right, doctor, here is something strange that happened to me. I don't know whether to call it a dream or synchronicity or what. The day we met, right after Beowulf ran toward you—"

"Ah, yes, the day you yelled at me," interrupted Angelika.

Rolf looked down and then turned his head toward Angelika. "I'll *never* yell at you again," he said slowly, putting his hand on her arm.

The intensity of his look made Angelika shiver. It was a moment she would remember for a long time afterward. She didn't know how to respond and was glad when Beowulf jumped off the davenport and gave a quick bark.

Dieter bounded into the room. "Well, at least you two aren't going at each other's throats again! Would you like to go out to dinner, or do you want me to whip something up in the kitchen?" he asked.

CHAPTER SEVENTEEN

TUESDAY morning Dean, Angela, and Lady drove to the clinic, with Lady sitting on the floor in front of Angela, while Angela petted her.

"That dog would be more comfortable in the back, you know." Dean glanced away from the road to look at Angela.

"I'd be more comfortable with her back there too, but then I couldn't pet her. I'm worried about the surgery."

"Why worry? Dr. Weiss said he's done several of these surgeries, and he seems competent enough. I think you're overreacting," Dean said dismissively.

Angela looked at him and frowned. She didn't know if Dean didn't take the surgery seriously enough, or if she was just a worrywart. "I don't think it's overreacting feeling worried about our baby!" She bent her head and kissed the dog, who was panting. Dean didn't answer, and the rest of the trip was driven in silence.

It was surgery day for Dr. Weiss, and although there were several people in the waiting room ahead of them, each client was in and out of the examining room in less than five minutes. Dr. Weiss called them in with a smile. Angela walked Lady in, and Dean followed. After kissing Lady on the forehead, she handed Dr. Weiss the leash.

"My wife is worried about the dog's surgery." Dean addressed Dr. Weiss.

Dr. Weiss looked at Angela and smiled, completely ignoring Dean. "I think a little concern about the dog you love is a good thing. But we'll take good care of her. No need to worry." He handed a paper to Angela. "Before you go, I need you to sign this. It's just routine."

Angela took the paper, glanced at it quickly, and signed the bottom. When she started to hand it back to Dr. Weiss, Dean spoke up. "Wait! I want to see it." She handed it to Dean, who held it for a minute and handed it back. "All right."

"We'll call you when she's ready for you to pick her up." Dr. Weiss turned to go.

"Can you call when she's out of surgery?" asked Angela.

Dr. Weiss, instead of being annoyed as she expected he might, turned around, gave her a big smile, and made a note on Lady's chart. "Sure. No problem. See you later." And he turned and stepped from the room, Lady following reluctantly.

Angela watched as Lady's stub of a tail disappeared out the door. She would have stayed there longer, biting on her knuckles, if Dean hadn't pulled her away. He put his hand on her shoulder and gently pushed her toward the door of the clinic.

It took them an hour to drive home, and Dean never stopped talking. She thought he did it to occupy her mind and keep her from worrying, but his going from one topic to the next with no pauses in between was just annoying. Although it did serve to keep her from worrying.

When they arrived home, Angela immediately checked their voicemail. It was empty.

Dean laughed when he saw her. "Angie, you gave them your cell number. They won't be calling on our home phone."

"I wanted to make sure, that's all." But for good measure, she pulled her cell phone out of her pocket and took a quick glance at it. Then she sat on the couch and tried to read a book. She'd read a page and then glance up at the clock. After a few minutes of that, it got to where she would read a paragraph and then glance up at the clock. And then just a sentence. She'd put the book in her lap and pull out her cell phone to make sure the battery was full.

Dean walked by once in a while and smirked at her actions. Finally, he couldn't help himself any longer. "Stop it, Angie! You're just acting stupid! They'll call when they call! Go water the garden or something!"

Nodding and frowning, Angela stood up and strolled outside. Her heart wasn't in it. Although she loved the garden, she didn't think she could focus while feeling so worried about Lady. But after a few minutes, she was consumed by the weeding, the new sprouts, and the beauty of the flowers she had insisted they plant. Dean had wanted to plant just a vegetable garden. Angela would have none of that. She wanted her flowers. As she was on her knees pulling out a persistent weed, a sound erupted from her pocket. Pulling out her cell phone as fast as she could, she answered it in a rushed voice.

By the time she pushed the *end* button on the phone,

she felt much relieved. It had been Dr. Weiss saying that Lady had come through the surgery fine and that the operation was a complete success. Lady would be ready for them to take her home in two hours. She was surprised that Dr. Weiss had called her personally instead of having one of his techs call to let her know, but his voice was calming and reassuring and that made her happy. And she liked his voice.

CHAPTER EIGHTEEN

WHEN Dr. Weiss hung up the phone after telling the woman that her dog was doing fine, he was smiling. She made him feel that way—the opposite of how Helen made him feel. And he wasn't going to feel guilty about it. He wasn't going to be unfaithful—never would be—but he deserved to be happy too. And if talking to and seeing the woman made him feel happy, well, so be it.

The surgery had gone well. It was the kind of surgery he liked: intricate and difficult. The dog's blood work appeared normal, anesthesia progressed normally, and when he started in on the eye, there had been no surprises. The surgery went smoothly, he had a fabulous time, and the dog came out of it fine. She was in recovery now, and by the time they arrived to pick her up, she should be almost fully awake. And he could hand the dog back and look at the woman's sparkling eyes as he did so. Yes, he couldn't deny that he would be happy to see her again.

As Dr. Weiss performed the other surgeries in the

following hour, he remained focused on what he needed to do. And when he had a bleeder during a spay, he handled it expertly, and the cat lost hardly any blood. What he found, though, was that any moment he had to spare, like before the surgery waiting for the tech to be ready, or just after surgery, or while he was washing his hands, he found that he anticipated—with delight—the woman's arrival. Seeing her. Talking to her.

Just after he finished removing a cast from a dog that had a broken leg, he was told that the woman—and her husband—were there to pick up the dog. He experienced an interesting sensation in his solar plexus. What was that? Excitement over seeing her? Whatever it was, he liked it. And he knew he liked her.

After feeling the leg to make sure it had healed properly, he put the dog back into the cage room and walked over to Lady's cage. She sat up groggily when she saw him. "How you doing, girl?" He lifted the latch of the cage, and the door opened. Lady walked out slowly, and Dr. Weiss knelt down and put on her collar and leash. "Let's go see your mom and dad, shall we?" Before standing up again, he turned Lady's head this way and that to get a good view of her eye.

Then he took a deep breath and walked to the examining room where the woman and her husband waited. Realizing he had a huge smile on his face, he tried to sober it up—not too much, though, he didn't want them thinking something was wrong—but less grin and a more professional bearing. He liked being professional, so he straightened his ever-present tie and entered the room.

The woman was leaning against the wall and looking at the floor. But the man saw him come in and said to the woman, "Angie, she's here."

Angie. So Angie was her name. She looked up with a smile—though the smile was for the dog, not for him—and held her hand out for the leash, then kneeled down to pet and kiss the dog, whose stub of a tail wagged.

"Lady came through surgery fine, and everything looks good. I removed the entire white spot, so she should have almost complete vision back when she heals." Dr. Weiss waited until the woman stood back up from petting the dog, then he continued. "She's a little sleepy yet, so don't give her any food for a few hours." Then he turned to one of his cabinets, opened it, searched through the contents, and pulled out a small bottle with a dropper cap. After writing something on the label, he held the bottle in one hand and put his other hand on Angie's arm. "Put a drop in her eye once in the morning and once in the evening. I'll need to see her again in a week." Noticing what he had done, he quickly pulled the hand away and stepped back. "Any questions?" he asked, flustered.

CHAPTER NINETEEN

Angelika was in the living room studying for her final exams. She had been at it for hours, so when the image of Rolf's intense look popped into her head, she gave in to it. Remembering the feel of his hand on her arm made her shiver. She touched her arm where he had touched it and gently stroked back and forth. Then she realized what she was doing and at once returned to her book.

But a few minutes later, Rolf interrupted her thoughts again. Why had he done that? And why did she care? What was it about him that drew her to him? Yes, that's it, isn't it, Angelika thought. She was drawn to him. It was difficult to admit to herself, but it was true. What in her subconscious would draw her to a man like that? A Nazi! And she a married woman. The whole idea of it made little sense to her. But since she was a student of psychotherapy, she would take it on herself to figure it out. That would be her real final exam.

The knock at the door shocked Angelika out of her

reverie. She closed her book and walked briskly to the front door. When she opened the front door, fear surged through her body. A tall Nazi officer stood there at attention. Her throat closed, her stomach tightened, and it took every bit of her courage not to slam the door in his face and run away. She couldn't speak.

Then she noticed a movement beside the man. She looked down and saw Wulfie sitting obediently, but his wagging tail gave him away. It wasn't until then that she realized the officer standing in front of her was Rolf. After leaning down to hug the dog, she invited them in and tried to get her heart to slow its frantic beating.

"For a minute there, Angelika, you looked like a scared Jew caught in the headlights!" Rolf laughed. He picked up a vase from a bookshelf and looked under it. "You're not hiding any Jews in here, I trust?"

"No, Rolf, just me," Angelika said, trying to sound casual. "Oh, and Freud. I've got him hidden upstairs in my bedroom, where he belongs." She smiled at the Nazi officer. Despite the horrible connotation behind the uniform, it made him look very handsome.

"Oh, you've never seen me in my uniform before, have you? That must have been why you looked so surprised. Usually I change before I drive over here, but today I left early. It's my birthday." He shrugged.

"Happy Birthday!" Angelika leaned forward to kiss him on the cheek. "I'll have to bake you a birthday cake!"

"I didn't think you cooked—" Rolf looked at her with a worried expression on his face.

"I don't. But my baking isn't bad. Don't worry, it will be palatable! I promise!" Angelika looked at him shyly. "Well, maybe I won't promise, but I'll try my best!" She gave Wulfie another hug and walked toward the kitchen.

"Angelika! Wait!" Rolf followed a few steps behind.

She turned around with her eyebrows up in question. "Yes?"

Rolf put his hand in the satchel that he wore around his shoulder and pulled out a book. "I brought you a present." He held the book out where she could reach it.

"It's *your* birthday and you brought *me* a present?" She took the book from him and stifled a gasp. "It's a book about Freud! It's forbidden!" Angelika recognized the book right away. It was one she already had which was kept hidden safely away in her underwear drawer upstairs. Still, she held it away from her body as if the forbidden part of it might be catching.

"You don't have to be afraid. Nobody will search your house. They know I stay here now." He motioned with his head. "Go ahead. Open it. You might learn something from it. And after you read it, maybe we can talk about it."

She opened the book and flipped to the table of contents—although she had already read it and knew exactly what would be there. Running her finger along the chapter titles, she nodded her head. Then she fanned through the pages before she closed it. "I'll read it later. Right now, I have to bake your cake!" Still holding the book, she headed toward the kitchen again and turned back to Rolf. "Thank you very much for this. I appreciate it."

A big grin spread across his face. "I thought you were going to throw it and me out!"

With a quick shake of her head, she said, "No. I'm just being cautious." She motioned toward Wulfie, and her eyes sparkled. "I wouldn't have thrown *him* out though." Then she disappeared into the kitchen leaving Rolf behind still smiling.

CHAPTER TWENTY

As they walked to the car, Angela holding onto Lady's leash, Dean looked at her. "He likes you, you know."

She shrugged her shoulders. "I like him too."

When they got to the car, Dean got behind the wheel as Angela opened the back door and helped a still sluggish Lady onto the seat. Then she slid in beside her and closed the door.

"What are you doing?" Dean looked in the rearview mirror.

"Sitting back here with Lady so she doesn't have to be alone. I think she's still disoriented, and I want to make her feel better."

"I'm not going to drive all the way home as your chauffeur!" He turned around to look at her. "Come on, get up here in front."

"Lady shouldn't be alone right now. But if it would make you more comfortable, I'd be happy to drive home and you can sit in the back with her." Angela opened the door.

Dean just huffed and made no move to exit the car. "How are we going to talk?"

Angela closed the door and buckled her seatbelt. "*We* don't talk, Dean. *You* do all the talking." Tired of doing all the listening, she felt now seemed a good time to address it. But Dean didn't say anything, he just started the car, backed it out of the parking space, and pulled out onto the main road. It didn't bother her that Dean didn't even try to defend himself. He knew what she said was true.

She petted Lady and spoke softly to her. Her eye looked much better—red from the surgery, but the white spot was gone. It was a good decision to have it removed. Lady was a good dog, and she deserved to see properly.

And then there was the good doctor. He had put his hand on her arm as he gave her the medicine. Dean never did that. And she missed that closeness. The only time Dean touched her was when they were intimate. That was sex, not closeness. It was like Dean couldn't handle the closeness. Obviously the doctor could. Angela wondered if he was married, then pushed the thought away. *She* was married, and she wasn't the fool-around type.

Dr. Weiss was very attractive. With his shaggy blond hair, blue eyes, and handsome build, she nodded her head, yes, he was very attractive. It was funny. The two days she had seen him—and she had no reason to believe it would be different any other time—he had not worn a lab coat. He had worn nice slacks, a dress shirt, and a tie. The first time she met him, it was a red tie with Dalmatians all over it. Today, it had been a blue tie with a lion on it. He looked professional—more like a CEO than a vet. But she knew that he loved animals—just the gentle way he acted with Lady confirmed that.

Next time she saw him, she'd have to ask him about Dalmatians. He didn't seem like a fancier of Dalmatians though. She wasn't sure what kind of dog would suit him, but not Dalmatians. There wasn't anything wrong with Dalmatians—they just didn't suit Dr. Weiss.

Angela started to laugh to herself, but caught herself before Dean noticed. She couldn't believe she thought she already knew what kind of dog would suit Dr. Weiss when she had only just met him. Then, after stifling the laugh, she furrowed her brow and thought for a minute. There was something about him that made her *feel* like she did know enough about him to make a judgment like that. It felt like she had *always* known him. And that thought gave her the shivers.

Lady had her eyes closed and her head on Angela's lap. Angela turned her attention to the dog. She stroked her back and sang softly to the dog.

"What are you doing?" demanded Dean.

"Making Lady feel better."

"Well, it's making me feel worse! Stop that off-key singing!"

"Lady doesn't mind. In fact, she likes it." Angela leaned forward, kissing Lady on the top of her head.

"*I* mind, so stop it!"

Ignoring Dean, Angela continued singing softly and petting Lady.

CHAPTER TWENTY-ONE

Dr. Weiss was horrified. Not in all the years that he had been a veterinarian had he ever *touched* a client like that. He had touched *no one* like that since he had been married—no one but Helen, that is. And she didn't even want him to touch her anymore in *any* way. That was beside the point. But how unprofessional can a doctor get! Ashamed of himself, he had to walk to the back of the clinic where the animals were to shake off his embarrassment before going into the next examining room. Then he realized that he hadn't looked to see which animal was being picked up next. When he spotted Megan, one of his techs, he strode up to her.

"Megan, can you check who gets picked up next? It would be the examination room on the right."

"Sure thing, Dr. Weiss." She disappeared through the door and was back less than a minute later.

"Puff. The cat that was spayed."

"Oh, yes." He headed toward the front. "Thanks, Megan," he said over his shoulder.

Dr. Weiss took a deep breath as he walked toward the examining room, composed himself, straightened his tie, and was about to walk into the room when he realized he had forgotten the cat. What was going on with him? He had never been this scattered in his life. Quickly returning to the cage room, he gently lifted the cat out, petted her until she purred, reached under her to feel for any blood seepage, found none, and returned to the examining room to give the owners the cat and the recovery instructions.

Three hours later after sending home all the animals scheduled to go home that day and taking care of the afternoon appointments, he could finally settle into his office. He had not had time to think about his faux pas since it happened, and thankfully so. Now he could sit back and think about *why* it happened.

Instead of checking his email first as he usually did, he slumped into his easy chair, looked at the dog-doctor clock without registering the time, and rested his chin on his fist. Why in the world had he done such a thing? While she was attractive and smart, he had run into plenty of women over the years who had been attractive and smart. That wasn't it. Angie seemed *interested* when he talked to her. Yes, he knew she was interested in what he had to say and not interested in *him*, but still, even that was better than being ignored or yelled at all the time when he was home.

There was something else too. Angie. Her name. There was something about her name that gave him the shivers. What was that about, he wondered. Dr. Weiss laughed at himself. What was he, in high school? It was ridiculous! A name making him feel that way. But it felt more complicated than that. It's like he *knew* the name already. Almost like he knew *her* already. Had they ever met before? No, there was no way he had ever met that woman before. He would remember. Surely he would remember a woman like that.

So what was it? He thought about Angie, shook off the feeling it gave him, and then thought about Helen. Angie. Helen. Angie. Helen. That was it. The contrast. It was the contrast between Angie and Helen. Whenever Helen looked at him, he felt like he had stepped into a freezer. When Angie looked at him, she was attentive and enthusiastic. Whenever Helen spoke to him, it was cruel and condescending. And when Angie spoke to him, it was soft and gentle like a warm summer breeze. And Helen *never* listened to him when he spoke. But Angie listened to every word, asked pertinent questions, and made him feel like he was a *person* again.

Wow! What a revelation that was! Helen dehumanized him with the way she spoke and acted toward him. Angie made him feel like a person again. A good person. A smart person. Someone *worth* listening to. And Helen made him feel *worthless*. That was the crux of it right there, wasn't it? Helen made him feel bad about himself, and Angie made him feel good about himself.

Dr. Weiss breathed more easily. There it was. He wasn't going mad after all. It wasn't that he really *liked* Angie—the thought of her name made him move his shoulders to shrug off the feeling it gave him—it was just the contrast between her and Helen. So the solution was much simpler than if he was actually *falling* for the woman. All he had to do was avoid Helen even more than he did now so he wouldn't feel the dehumanizing looks and the sounds of her voice—so he wouldn't feel the contrast. There was no way he would divorce Helen and let Carla down.

CHAPTER TWENTY-TWO

INTENT on stirring the batter, Angelika didn't notice the footsteps coming toward her until arms closed around her waist. She felt a kiss on the back of her head. For a strange moment, she thought the kiss was from Rolf. So when she turned, she felt a surprising shock to find that the arms around her were Dieter's. She gave him a quick kiss on the lips and turned back to the batter, hoping he wouldn't notice her shock.

"What are you doing?" Dieter released his arms from around her. "I thought the kitchen was my domain."

"I'm making a cake for Rolf. Today's his birthday! Didn't you know? You should have told me." She glanced at him and then returned to finish her stirring.

"I didn't think it mattered." He stepped up to her and whispered in her ear. "I thought he was just another Nazi to you."

She turned to face Dieter. "He's more than that." Suddenly feeling like she had said something wrong, she turned back to the batter and added, "He's your brother

82

—my brother-in-law."

Dieter laughed. "You didn't even know about him until a couple of months ago."

Angelika shrugged and poured the batter into a pan. "Excuse me," she said, pushing past him toward the oven.

Dieter walked away and then turned to her, holding up the book Rolf had given her. "Angelika! You need to put this away! *He'll* see it." He whispered just loud enough for her to hear.

She smiled at him. "*He* gave it to me. Mine is still hidden upstairs."

Putting the book down, Dieter walked up to her. "*He* gave it to you? It's a forbidden book! It's about a *Jew*!" He looked at her with fear and doubt in his eyes.

She put one hand on his shoulder, and with the other took the book out of his hands and put it back on the counter. "Don't worry! He told me that no one would search the house because they know that he stays here now." When Dieter still looked doubtful, she continued. "It's all right, Dieter. Really. He just wanted to give it to me, so we could talk about it."

"Maybe I should go talk to him." Dieter crossed in front of her and slid out the door toward the living room.

As Angelika cleaned the kitchen, she heard their voices in the other room. Although she couldn't make out any words, it was a constant buzz of conversation. Let them deal with it. She felt comfortable that Rolf had given her the forbidden book. When she thought of it, she realized she was comfortable with Rolf. The man who had once been the scary Nazi—the enemy—had now become a friend. Nodding her head brought back to mind when Dieter said he thought Rolf was just another Nazi to her, and she had said he was more than that and then added that he was her brother-in-law. But before she added the brother-in-law part, she had felt uncomfortable saying that he was more than that.

Because he was. Angelika could see that now. He did mean more to her than just another Nazi. He meant a lot more to her. The thought made her put her hand on her chest and lean back against the counter. How could that be? She was in love with Dieter, wasn't she? Was she? She *loved* him; she knew that. But was she *in love* with him? Or had he just been convenient, steadfast, reliable? Although she thought—had always thought—that Dieter was all she ever wanted in a man, now she wondered. They never talked about the things that mattered to her —like her interest in psychology. He always asked how she was doing in school, but they never talked about her studies.

And she and Rolf did. He was interested in psychology and wanted to discuss it with her. Rolf even gave her that book and said after she read it they could talk about it. If he had known how much that meant to her, he never would have given her that book. *Now* look what he had done. He made her realize what was missing in her relationship with Dieter. Intelligent conversation. Dieter was smart and all—an attorney—but they never discussed anything of import. He couldn't discuss his cases with her, not that a tax attorney would have interesting cases, but still, they could have discussed something interesting—even books they had read. Except they never read the same kind of books, and his books didn't interest her, and her books didn't interest him.

But Rolf gave her a book she had already read and

was already intrigued by. He must have already read it or how could they talk about it? And he liked talking about psychology—about Freud and Jung. Not to mention he was gorgeous and even more so in his Nazi uniform. She hated the connotation of his uniform, but it fit him well. And him owning Wulfie, the dog she loved, didn't hurt anything either. Dieter would never let her have a dog. Yes, she had to admit it. She was developing feelings for Rolf. Now what was she going to do?

CHAPTER TWENTY-THREE

WATCHING Lady playing in the field behind their house gave Angela great pleasure. Although since Lady had hurt her eye, Angela now walked her with a leash through the bushes and brambles. Lady was cooperative about having the eyedrops put in her eyes, and she was recovering nicely. Angela was certain that her first check-up since surgery would confirm that. Dean's job had finally become full-time, so he wouldn't be driving with them to the vet clinic in Berlin. Although she hated to admit it, Angela felt grateful that he wouldn't be going. Putting up with his negativity had grown more and more tiresome, and she wouldn't mind seeing Dr. Weiss alone anyway.

That thought made her catch her breath. Alone with Dr. Weiss? What was she thinking? She was a married woman! Unhappily married, maybe, but still married. Well, she wouldn't be alone with him anyway. There were people all over that clinic—technicians walking by the door constantly—and besides, Lady would be there.

At that moment Lady ran up to her and dropped the ball at her feet. Angela grabbed the ball and threw it as hard as she could down the field.

As Lady charged after the ball, Angela returned to her thoughts. What was it about Dr. Weiss that made her think these thoughts about him? Yes, he was attractive and smart, but she had met attractive and smart men at her job, and they did nothing for her. What was it about him? She took a deep breath and let the answer come to her. He listened to her. Could it be that simple? Dean rarely listened to her; he was always too busy blathering on and on about whatever it was he was interested in. Hadn't Dean been a good listener when they first got together? She thought he was, so what happened? Or was it just that she was so enamored of him that she didn't realize that he did all the talking and she did all the listening? Frowning, she suspected that was closer to the truth.

Lady came running back up and rubbed against Angela, looking up into her eyes with love. Angela sank down on the ground hugging Lady to her. "You're such a good girl, Lady. I love you so much!" The big dog flopped across her lap and made her laugh. "You're too big to be a lap dog, Lady!" But Angela kept stroking the dog and remembered back to when she was a puppy, so many years ago.

She had been wild—wilder than anyone could imagine! The breeder had nicknamed her the "wild one," and she definitely lived up to her name. When they first brought her home, she would run around the house in circles, as fast as she could. That went on for weeks. It was like nothing would calm her down or wear her out. Dean hated her. All he ever talked about was getting rid of her.

And Angela loved her. Lady may have been a horrible handful, but she was *real*. She liked having someone pet her, and she liked the attention. Lady made Angela feel loved. Dean never made Angela feel loved. Again, he must have in the beginning, or she wouldn't have married him. And although he did say "I love you" to her every day, it still didn't make her feel loved.

So Angela remembered when she had made the decision back then. If Dean said Lady had to go, then Angela would go with her. And there had been no doubt in her mind. It was what she wanted. It was more important for her to keep Lady than to stay married to Dean. What surprised her at the time was how easily the decision had come. One would think that choosing to leave the man you are married to *for a dog* would require restless nights and painful and confusing contemplation. But there had been none of that. She had been sitting watching Lady chew on a toy, and it had just come to her. Lady over Dean. No second thoughts.

It had never come to that. Lady had calmed down eventually, and Dean had never given her that ultimatum. When Lady had settled down, though, was when she almost died. That's when Dean realized that not only was Lady not as bad as his constant complaints made her seem, but he actually did love her after all. There were times, though, that Angela wished Dean *had* given her an ultimatum. It would be better than the miserable state of their marriage now. Angela shrugged her shoulders. They'd had rough spots in their marriage before and had gotten through them. Maybe they would get through them again. Her thoughts flashed to Dr. Weiss. And maybe they wouldn't.

CHAPTER TWENTY-FOUR

Dr. Weiss managed to stay out of Helen's way the rest of that week. He thought that was the reason that he hadn't thought too much about the woman, Angie. Too much was relative, he knew that, but at least he didn't think of her every waking minute, and he thought that was a plus. Sunday morning, he awoke early, slipped quietly out of bed so as not to wake Helen, gulped down a quick cup of coffee and strode happily out to his garden, the dog Wolf following him.

His garden meant the world to him. The colors, the fragrances—when he was working in his garden, it transported him to a different world, a kinder world. As he breathed in the fresh scent of clean soil and felt it in his fingers, a wave of happiness engulfed him. He was almost as much at peace as when he was at the clinic. Glancing over at the house, he shook his head. No, when he was here—at the house—he was always waiting for another explosion from Helen. She could get angry and resentful of the simplest things.

Dr. Weiss remembered the first year he had his garden. They had moved into the house in late spring, and when the snow finally melted, he prepared the soil. When the flowers emerged, he was so proud of them. And although he loved looking at them where they grew, he decided that he would sacrifice a few to give Helen a fresh bouquet of beautiful, fragrant flowers. He had bought the perfect vase for her, carefully cut the stems, and then with a huge smile on his face presented them to her. She shoved the vase back into his hands so fast, he had almost dropped it on the floor.

"They've got bugs on them! I don't want them in my kitchen! They'll get on the food! Yuck! Take those filthy things out to the garage where they belong."

Thinking of it now still made his stomach sink and his head ache. It had disappointed him so much when she couldn't share the flowers' beauty with him. It had never bothered him that she didn't want to *work* in the garden —he preferred working alone out there anyway—but when she had rejected his recent conciliatory gift of a beautiful vase and the even more beautiful roses, that had deeply disturbed him. That day, after she did that, he had immediately gotten into his car—with the vase full of flowers—and brought them to the clinic where he could enjoy them there. Even when all the techs and clerks had commented on how beautiful the flowers were, it didn't take away the pain of Helen's rejection.

When he found himself rubbing his chest over his heart with his soil-encrusted hand, he realized the pain of that moment still lived within him. He sighed and dug back into the dirt planting a fresh bulb. Stopping for a moment and gazing into the sky, he thought back to the previous year reflectively. Last year had been even worse.

Maybe not worse, but at least as bad.

There was a rose bush in the front of the house that he cared for tenderly. Last year, its blooms had been so beautiful that all the neighbors stopped by to tell him how wonderful they were. Cars would slow down and people get out just to look. One man commented how he should enter the roses in the county fair. He was an older gent and said he had won in years past, and that these roses were better than anything he had ever grown.

Dr. Weiss had felt so excited about the prospect of winning at the county fair. He filled out the application and couldn't wait to see if he would win. Helen, however, thought differently about it and screamed at him daily to abandon his stupid idea. That's what she called it, stupid.

"You're not really going to enter those ugly flowers at the fair, are you? Those aren't prize-winning roses. You're just deluding yourself that you could ever win! Don't be an idiot!"

He had stopped talking about them, but didn't cancel his entry. As the time for the fair grew nearer, her real motive came out. "Come on, Ralph, don't enter those flowers. Even if you win—especially if you win—people will look at you like you're a *farmer*. I hate that people might think I'm married to a *farmer*." She had said it with disdain, thrown her dish cloth into the sink, and stomped out of the room.

So that was it. His flowers might embarrass her even if he won—*especially* if he won. He had taken pride in that. She may have thought his flowers were ugly or she may have just been saying that, but she did admit that he might win. Shaking his head, he tamped the dirt down around the bulb. He'd never forget what happened next.

When he didn't withdraw his application, and with just two days before the event, he had come home one day to find every single rose on the bush gone. Cut out. When he had questioned her about it, she shook her head and said some neighborhood kids must have done it. He was heartbroken, but not half as heartbroken as he was the following day when he found them in the garbage can. They were right on top. She hadn't even tried to hide them.

CHAPTER TWENTY-FIVE

GERMANY 1940

SEVERAL weeks passed with Angelika going to school and working in her garden. She missed Wulfie, and thinking about Wulfie made her think about Rolf, whom she had been doing her best not to think about. It was just a schoolgirl crush, that's all. She was in love with Dieter, and Dieter was her husband, and that was that. Rolf was just a handsome stranger. A handsome stranger who just happened to be a Nazi! How could she forget that? Her future was with Dieter. Angelika could enjoy her conversations with Rolf—the Nazi—but her place was here, with Dieter. He had signed up with the Nazi Party—as had she—because he had to. Rolf was in it of his own accord; he even worked for them!

But did she have to keep reminding herself that she was in love with Dieter? And if it needed reminders like that, was it true? She sighed, dusted off her hands, and walked into the house. After washing off the dirt from the garden, she stepped out of the bathroom, heard Dieter's voice, and followed the sound into the kitchen.

93

Angelika threw her arms around him.

"I love you, Dieter." But even as she said it, she wondered if it *was* true.

"What's that about, huh, Angelika?" Dieter turned around and returned the hug.

"I just wanted you to know, that's all." She pulled away from him and forced a smile on her lips.

"Ah, little brother, you look very becoming in that apron." Rolf had appeared from nowhere and stood in the doorway looking in.

Seeing Wulfie by his side, Angelika knelt down and beckoned the dog to come to her. He obliged, lay down at her feet, and flipped over so she could rub his stomach. "That's my boy, Wulfie. That's my boy."

"Beowulf! Come!" Rolf pointed to his feet, and the dog sat down at attention. "He is not *your* boy, Angelika. He is *my* boy."

Angelika stood, marched up to Rolf, and put her hand on the dog's head. "If you have to *order* him to come to you, I don't think that's proof. Why don't you see who he would go to without any *orders*, or don't you have the nerve for that?" She marched past him into the other room, sitting on the edge of the davenport where she could still hear the conversation in the kitchen.

"That was harsh, Rolf. She wasn't going to take the dog away from you!"

"I know. I'll apologize. I'm just on edge right now."

The conversation continued, but Rolf had begun to whisper to Dieter, and Angelika couldn't hear a thing. She moved toward the other edge of the davenport, where she usually sat, and picked up one of her textbooks.

Several minutes later, Rolf and Wulfie walked to the

94

living room. "I'm sorry, Angelika. I have a lot on my mind. You are welcome to pet the dog any time."

"Thanks, Rolf." She opened her arms and without saying a word beckoned the dog to her. Wulfie rushed over and once again flopped onto his back for her to scratch his tummy.

"I still don't understand what goes on between you and that dog. He's never acted that way with me or with anyone else." Rolf shook his head and moved toward the front door to retrieve the luggage that he had left there.

Angelika was still petting Wulfie when Rolf returned and sat next to her on the davenport. "Here. I brought you something." He handed her a book.

"Another one? You already gave me a book."

Rolf shook his head. "I overheard you and Dieter talking that you already have that book. So this is a new one. Just out. By Jung." He smiled at her. "It's even legal!"

Angelika took the book and flipped through it. "Thank you, Rolf. I appreciate this."

He reached over and pointed to the table of contents. "Take a look at these chapters. Dreams, naturally, but look at these others: alchemy, astrology, archetypes, individuation, world religion, his theory of synchronicity, mythology, and the collective unconscious." Rolf tapped the book with his forefinger. "This book is ahead of its time. Jung is ahead of his time. I think you'll like it, and I look forward to discussing it all with you—there might even be something new about his theory of synchronicity."

Before she had a chance to answer him, he abruptly stood up, grabbed her hand, and pulled her up in front of him. "Angelika," he paused and then put his hand on her cheek, "Angie—"

"Nobody calls me Angie." But she said it without anger and put her hand on top of his hand. They looked into each other's eyes.

"Angie, I—"

From the kitchen, they heard Dieter call out. "Who's ready for dinner?"

By the time he appeared in the doorway, Rolf was walking away and Angelika had sat back down on the davenport, her hand on her cheek where Rolf's had been. She could still feel the warmth of his touch.

CHAPTER TWENTY-SIX

A week passed, and when it was time to take Lady back to the veterinarian, Angela loaded her in the front seat of the car and took off down the road. She was going alone this time, because Dean was working. Angela didn't realize how much she looked forward to going alone until she noticed how uplifted she felt as she drove to Berlin. Although she talked to Lady during the whole drive, her mind was elsewhere. It was on Dr. Weiss, where she knew it shouldn't be.

The parking lot was full, as usual, because Dr. Weiss had a large practice. The waiting room would be full, too, she knew. She grabbed Lady's leash, helped her out of the car, and walked inside the building. After checking them in at the reception area, she sat at the far end of the room, trying to stay away from any other animals. But it was too busy for that. It didn't matter, though, she realized. Lady normally wasn't good with other dogs, but in the waiting room, she always ignored them. Perhaps she was just nervous about her surroundings. Angela felt

97

nervous, too, like she was on a first date or something. How ridiculous, she thought, and picked up a *Smithsonian* magazine to leaf through.

It didn't seem ridiculous, though, when he stepped from the end examining room and called Lady's name, because she lit up like a Christmas tree. A smile spread across her face as she walked across the room toward Dr. Weiss. He was wearing a pink pressed shirt, and a black tie with multi-colored kittens playing on it.

"Hello, Mrs.—" He glanced at Lady's chart.

"Angie. Just Angie."

"Angie it is," he returned her smile, and she almost sank at his feet right then. "How is our girl?" He knelt, took Lady's face in his hands, and looked into the eye that he had operated on. "The eye's doing well. You've been administering the drops?"

"Yes, of course." She knelt down on the other side of Lady so she could look into his blue eyes.

"It looks like it; I just wanted to make sure. Do you have enough for two more weeks—that's when I need to see her again—or should I give you more?" He raised his eyebrows and tilted his body toward the cabinet where he had gotten the drops before.

"I have plenty. Lady's good about letting me put them in her eyes, so I haven't wasted any."

"That's good." Dr. Weiss nodded longer than was necessary. "So, what do you feed pretty Lady here?" He stepped back, leaned against the counter behind him, and crossed his arms over his chest.

"A good premium food. One without grain." When he pursed his lips together, nodded, and said nothing, she added, "Don't you agree with the whole grain-free idea?"

He uncrossed his arms, smiled, and took a step forward. "I didn't say that. For me, the jury is still out."

"Well, personally, I'm on a paleo diet, so it's no grains for me, either." She shrugged.

"Really?" He took another step forward and put his hands on the examining table between them. "That's the one that is supposed to mimic the diet from paleolithic times?"

"Yes, exactly. The diet humans had for two and a half million years—no grains. Farming and eating grain has only been around for ten thousand years."

"And you don't think ten thousand years is enough time for the human body to adjust to grains?" Dr. Weiss smiled at her.

"Not when they cause distress and inflammation in our bodies. If the human body had adjusted to grains, they wouldn't cause inflammation, do you think?" She tilted her head and shrugged her shoulders.

He nodded. "Sounds like a good point. I'll have to look into that."

"It's the same with dogs," she continued. "It causes inflammation in dog's bodies too. I just read that 90 percent of the pathology of an animal is caused by what they eat. Do you agree with that?"

Dr. Weiss shook his head. "No, I don't agree with that at all. There are many causes, and I think nutrition is on the lower end of the scale."

"Said like a true traditional vet." She smiled at him.

"Oh, you believe in all that *alternative* medicine, then?"

"Yes, I do. It's been around much longer than the new medication-driven medicine."

He turned toward the door. "I need to go now, but I've enjoyed our conversation—the think-talking. I don't get

99

that very often."

She nodded at him and turned serious. "Yeah, me, either."

"Make an appointment for two weeks from now, and I'll see you then. Bye Mrs.—I mean, Angie." He smiled and strode out the door.

"Goodbye, Dr. Weiss." Angela took a deep breath, steadied herself, and led Lady through the door.

CHAPTER TWENTY-SEVEN

Dr. Weiss would have liked to talk to the woman longer, but he knew he had clients bulging out of the waiting room that needed attention. It would be many hours later when everyone had left the clinic that he could relax in his office. Flopping down in his easy chair, he exhaled slowly and began to think of her. It didn't faze him that he didn't check his email first as he usually did.

His only focus right now was to think about the conversation they had. A great conversation. When did he last have a thinking conversation with Helen? He chuckled to himself at the absurdity of it all. Who was he kidding? When did he last have any conversation with his wife that didn't involve one of them—usually her—screaming? The last time they had an intellectual conversation that stimulated him would have been years and years ago—way, way before the marital strife that had plagued them for so long now.

Where did he go wrong with his marriage? He

101

brought in a good income to support her and the children. She could have anything she wanted just by asking. And he made enough that she didn't need to work, as so many wives did today. She had complete freedom. So where did he go wrong? As he shrugged his shoulders, the thought crossed his mind that maybe he hadn't gone wrong, maybe she had, but he discarded that thought immediately, because he wasn't the kind of man who blamed his troubles on someone else. Dr. Weiss had gone wrong somewhere, but for the life of him, he couldn't figure out where it was.

While leaving those depressing thoughts of his marriage behind, the scene in the examining room with *Angie* came back to mind. Why did even her name make him feel giddy? It was as if he had known her before, but he knew that he had never met her prior to the day she and her husband walked into the office. And the conversation! They may not agree, but still, he *liked* it. He liked discussions like that and wanted more of them. Dr. Weiss wanted many more of them—but how would that happen? There was no way he would wish the dog sick so Angie would come in more often. And after the two week appointment, there would be one more in a month, and then the dog should be fine.

A sigh escaped his lips. A sad sigh. Angie was married, and he was married. That was the end of *that*. Any fantasies he might have of them sharing more of those kinds of thinking-conversations were just that—fantasies. They could talk when she brought the dog back in two weeks, and then again a month after that, and that would be the end of that fantasy.

And she believed in alternative vet care, which meant that she came to him because he was an eye specialist.

He may never see her again. Sighing again, he resigned himself to a life of marital discord and loneliness. Dr. Weiss had never admitted that to himself before, but it was true. How can a person be lonely when they're married? Nodding his head, he put his hands on the arms of the chair and boosted himself up. That was the worst kind of loneliness. And how Helen had been treating him? Reprehensible. What had he done to deserve that?

Still, he had signed on the dotted line "till death do us part," and he would honor that contract. And what about Carla? What would she think of him if she thought he was considering leaving her mother? Oh, no, he could never risk the disapproval and condemnation in her eyes when she looked at him. He already had to endure the disdain in Helen's eyes.

The phone rang, and because he had just been thinking of Carla, he thought it was her and answered it with a smile in his voice.

"Ralph! Is this you, Ralph?" a voice shouted.

"Yes, it's me. What is it, Helen?" Dr. Weiss recognized the voice, but she didn't often call him at the office.

"Carla's in the hospital! Can you leave right away?"

"Is she okay? What happened? Should I pick you up?"

"No, you shouldn't pick me up, you idiot! I'm already here!" And the phone went dead.

CHAPTER TWENTY-EIGHT

GERMANY 1940

DINNER felt like an hour of tension to Angelika as she and Rolf made an effort not to look into each other's eyes. She ate fast hoping to get away from the table, but Dieter never noticed her—nor Rolf's—discomfort and kept telling story after story. The only thing she could do was wait. Her favorite dessert, chocolate cake with chocolate frosting, even had to be forced down because she felt so—so—what? She couldn't even describe how she felt at that moment. Out of place would be the closest she could come. Because it was as if her whole world had just crumbled around her. The world she knew, anyway.

Midway through dessert, Rolf stood abruptly, announced that he had reading to catch up on, and walked stiffly from the room, but not before glancing at Angelika and raising his eyebrows almost imperceptibly. She knew Dieter hadn't noticed, because he kept going on and on with his stories. And going. And going. Finally, she stood up.

"Dieter, I'm going to the other room to study. Sorry about that."

He put a fake look of pain on his face. "You mean you're not going to clean up tonight?" Frowning, he continued, "I have to do all the cooking *and* the cleaning? That's not fair."

She smiled and tousled his hair, knowing he was kidding. Although that was the general rule—he cooked, she cleaned—there were times when he did it all and didn't seem to mind.

"I need to go study. You know I have final exams next week."

He put his arm around her waist and pulled her close to him. "I know. I don't mind." Taking her hand in his, he kissed it, before she walked away.

Feeling guilty, she sank down heavily into the chair and picked up her textbook. Angelika turned to where her bookmark was and turned the pages without reading them. All she could see on the pages of the book—or anywhere else she looked—was Rolf's blue eyes boring into hers. And the slight raise of his eyebrows when he left the table made her wonder if that meant they weren't finished yet. The thought terrified her and thrilled her at the same time. She unconsciously reached up and put her hand on her face where Rolf's hand had been. Closing her eyes, she imagined that the hand on her face *was* his.

An hour later and still on the same page of the book, she found that she couldn't get Rolf's eyes and Rolf's touch out of her mind. She couldn't focus on anything else. Dieter walked out of the kitchen and into the living room. Angelika stiffened and then turned another page of the book before she looked up to meet his eyes. Feeling embarrassed, she said nothing.

Dieter smiled at her. "You ready for a break? I thought I could call Rolf down, and the three of us could play cards."

Agitated about having to see Rolf and Dieter again in the same room, she quickly said, "No, no, don't call Rolf. The exams will be tough this year. I still need to study."

"Oh, come on, Angelika, you could use a break." He turned, walked to the staircase, and called out, "Rolf! Rolf! Come down and let's play cards."

"Dieter, I told you no. I need to study."

She heard Rolf at the top of the staircase and listened as he walked down and into the room. Not looking up, she flipped through the pages of her book.

"What's all the shouting about, little brother?"

Wulfie walked over to Angelika and licked her hand. When she didn't respond to him, he placed one of his paws in her lap trying to get her attention. When she still didn't respond to him, he yipped quietly and tried to nuzzle her.

"Wulfie, leave me alone! I need to study!" Wulfie slunk away with his tail between his legs.

"She rejected my dog? She does need to study then. Why don't we leave her alone, brother? Your wife is serious about her work." Rolf kneeled down to pet Wulfie.

Dieter fell into a chair across from Angelika. "Oh, Angelika, you already know all that boring stuff backwards and forwards. You can take a break."

"Dieter, I told you I need to study. I have final exams this coming week. Do I need to lock myself in the library to get some quiet in here?" Angelika flipped more pages of the book and ran her hand down the page like she was studying.

Dieter sighed and stood back up. "Well, can I ask you one question while I'm thinking about it? I can probably get some time off, so where do you want to go when school ends? Once you finish your exams, we'll go somewhere and have some fun."

Without looking up and without having thought about it before, the answer came to her in an instant. "Some friends and I have already planned to go to Paris to celebrate. Maybe you and I can go another time."

With her peripheral vision, she saw Dieter shrug and walk back into the kitchen. She heard Rolf take Wulfie to the back door. And Angelika was once more alone with the thoughts that haunted her.

CHAPTER TWENTY-NINE

AFTER paying for her visit and making Lady's next appointment at the reception desk, Angela led Lady out the front door, through the entryway, and then out into the bright sunshine. Quickly scanning the parking lot to see if anyone was leaving their car and coming her way, she put her hand on her chest and leaned against the closed door. Butterflies! She had butterflies in her stomach after talking to Dr. Weiss! How long had it been since she'd had butterflies with Dean? Too long to remember—if she ever had them at all. She heard someone open the inside door, so she gathered herself and headed across the parking lot toward her car.

Once Lady was in the car, she walked around to the other side and slid into the driver's seat. Taking a deep breath, she tried to calm down. Angela didn't want to drive when she was feeling like this. It had been an exhilarating conversation! Not everyone might think so, but she loved talking about anything related to health and medicine. In another life, she may have chosen to be a doctor—or a vet. In this life, however, health and medicine would just be a hobby. But she loved talking about it! And he seemed engaged, too—until he had to leave, that is.

She took a deep breath, started the car, and took another deep breath before putting it into gear and backing up. As she drove onto the highway toward home, Angela was starting to feel herself again. Not that she wanted to —she liked the excited feeling she had when she was around Dr. Weiss. But she was married. Then she had another thought. That didn't have to be permanent! It wasn't the first time in their troubled marriage she had thought about leaving Dean, divorcing him. If she could feel like this every day, have conversations like this every day, what a life that would be!

As she drove, she glanced over at Lady. "Lady," she said aloud, "how would you feel about having a new Daddy—a different Daddy?" Angela frowned, thought for a second, then spoke to the dog again. "Lady?" The dog looked over at her. "Would you go with me if I left, or would you stay with your Daddy?" Anytime she ever spoke to Lady, she referred to herself as "Mommy" and Dean as "Daddy." It wasn't just because the dog was so important in her life, but because she and Dean had no children. She thought it might be that need in every woman to feel like someone should call her "Mommy."

When she thought about it, if she chose to leave Dean, she wouldn't be leaving the Dean she married. She would be leaving the Dean that he had become, the Dean that she didn't like very much. The Dean she had married was fun to be with, but the new Dean was no fun at all. He had become so negative when he couldn't find a job, and even after getting the job, he would still complain all the time. It was like nothing was ever right for him. He was unhappy with everything. It made her wonder if she was one of the things that wasn't right for him—one of the things he was unhappy about. Because she was certainly unhappy with him.

Her thoughts drifted back to Dr. Weiss. She wondered if he was married. Because if she decided to leave Dean, it wouldn't do her any good if Dr. Weiss was married. He didn't wear a ring, but through her single years, she realized that meant nothing. Men didn't always wear rings, especially men who worked with their hands in their respective professions. How would she find out? She couldn't just come out and ask him. That would be terribly inappropriate. Could she ask the receptionist? No. That would also be inappropriate. Did she really want to know?

That was another question to consider. Although she and Dean were what one might call "unhappily married," still, he was her husband, and there was a certain amount of security in that. Dr. Weiss was an unknown. Dean was familiar. Their life was familiar, and although not happy, it was at least comfortable. It was what she had known for years now. She knew Dean well and knew everything about him. She didn't like everything she knew about him, but their relationship was comfortable. Not happy, not exciting, but comfortable and familiar. Would she consider leaving that security for something unknown? Angela would have to think more about that one.

CHAPTER THIRTY

DR. Weiss was so worried abut Carla that he could hardly drive. Why hadn't Helen even told him if Carla was all right or not? As a veterinarian, Dr. Weiss was fully aware that "in the hospital" could be anything from a deep gash that needed stitches to something that was a life and death situation. Now he had to wait the ten minutes—or less if he could manage—that it would take him to get to the hospital. He just had to be careful not to get a ticket, because that would delay him even more.

While he drove, he wondered about the possibilities. The best possible scenario would be a minor injury from after-school sports. The worst would be a car accident on the way home. He glanced at the clock on the dashboard. Helen was already at the hospital, so it would have happened at least thirty minutes—maybe sixty minutes—ago. That didn't narrow it down at all. It could still be either possibility, and in reality, it could be a hundred other things that could have happened. Forcing himself not to think of any horrible misfortunes that might have befallen Carla, he pulled into the hospital parking lot.

He parked the car and ran toward the emergency room, locking the door with his remote on the way. Since Helen hadn't told him where Carla was, he had to assume the emergency room. Even if that was wrong, they could direct him to where she was. Dr. Weiss burst through the outer emergency room doors, making everyone in the room look up at him. There was a woman at the desk telling the clerk what was wrong with her. Dr. Weiss looked frantically around and finally couldn't wait any longer.

"I'm sorry to interrupt. But is my daughter here? Carla Weiss? Please tell me!"

"I'm sorry, sir. You must wait until I finish with this person," said the clerk in a bored, nasally tone.

"Oh, God." Dr. Weiss walked around in circles, not knowing what else to do.

A woman came out from the back office and stepped up to the counter. "Dr. Weiss?"

"Yes! Yes!"

"Your daughter came in with a broken ankle. She's just been transferred from surgery to recovery. So you can't see her for a while now."

Dr. Weiss looked at the woman with gratitude. "Thank you so much." He shook his head. "Thank you so much. I appreciate you telling me this more than I can say."

"No problem, Dr. Weiss. You may not recognize me, but you're my cat's vet, and I appreciate very much how well you take care of her." She turned to return to the office from where she had come.

Dr. Weiss, his thoughts clearer since he knew that Carla was okay, looked at the woman as she walked away. "Mrs. Benton! I'm sorry I didn't recognize you! Thank you again!" Mrs. Benton turned, smiled, and continued into the back office.

He walked briskly down the hallway toward the windowless recovery room, already knowing that they wouldn't allow him entry. Frowning at the closed door, he made his way toward the front desk thinking that he could find out more information.

"Excuse me. I'm the father of Carla Weiss. Can you tell me her status right now, please?"

The woman looked up and appraised him before returning to her computer and keying in the name. "Carla Weiss is in recovery right now, due to go to her room in about thirty minutes."

"What room will that be, please?"

She glanced back at the screen. "Room 242." Without another word, she returned to what she was doing.

"Thank you," said Dr. Weiss as he walked away.

Thirty minutes. Although he wanted to be there when Carla returned from recovery, he did *not* want to get there so early that Helen would have time to berate him. He got enough of that at home. And thirty minutes sounded a little premature anyway. He estimated at least sixty minutes. Regardless, he wasn't going to Room 242 this early and take a chance on seeing Helen.

For the next twenty minutes, he walked randomly around the hospital, looking at the babies, stopping in a waiting room now and then to pick up a magazine and leaf through it. Then he cautiously walked by Room 242, careful not to tarry too long in the doorway. He did not want Helen to even see him walk by the room. She would start in on him immediately; he knew that. Using his peripheral vision, he saw that she was not looking out the door. After proceeding down the hallway for a few more steps, he turned around and retraced his steps more slowly. The bed was empty. Carla wasn't back yet.

As he walked by the nurses' station, a pretty nurse with short blonde hair called out to him. "Dr. Weiss! Your daughter's room is back that way." She pointed in the direction from where he had just come. "And your wife is in there waiting."

He knew her. She was a smart, young woman who took good care of her dog, a Scottish Terrier. He nodded to her. "Yes, Miss Crandall, I know that's the room. I thought I'd wait out here for a while." He gave her a quick smile and shrugged.

"Oh. Yes. I understand." She raised her eyebrows and gave him a knowing look.

Helen had undoubtedly shown her wrath to the girl. Nobody was safe these days. She took it out on everyone, not just him. Although she didn't much yell at the kids—not that she saw them that often. They had lives of their own. And at their age, they should.

Thirty minutes later, he saw a nurse wheeling a wheelchair down the hallway. It was Carla! He ran toward her. "Carla! Carla! Are you all right?"

She still seemed groggy, but she answered. "I'm fine, Daddy. I'm fine."

The nurse wheeled her into Room 242, and Dr. Weiss followed.

As soon as Helen saw him—before she even acknowledged Carla—she yelled at him. "Ralph! What took you so long? I've been sitting her alone for an hour wondering where you were!"

The nurse was helping Carla into the bed, but Carla leaned over and poked her head around the nurse.

"Daddy? Why do you let her talk to you like that?"

Later, he would think it was only the residual of the anesthesia drugs talking. But it got him to thinking. Why *did* he let her talk to him like that?

CHAPTER THIRTY-ONE

THREE days into her final exams and Angelika still had found no one to go with her to Paris. Most of her good friends lived with their parents and needed permission first. Two of her friends weren't interested, two were still waiting for an answer from their parents, and one hadn't gotten back to her. Her only exam on Thursday was early in the morning, and her plan was to leave right after that. If no one would go with her, she had already decided that she would go by herself.

No, she wouldn't tell that to Dieter. He would never consent. He would insist that she delay long enough for him to get time off. And that wasn't an option. It was almost better if no one went with her. That way she could spend the entire time on the train thinking about the complications in her life and what she would do about it.

The more she thought about it, though, she realized that it would be much better to go by herself. One reason she had decided to go was to get away by herself. Asking her friends was because she had told Dieter that she was going with them. Nodding her head, she hoped that the two friends' parents would say no, and that the last friend who hadn't responded yet would also say no. Then she could get what she needed—some space for thinking. Alone. Angelika knew now that she needed to go alone.

By the end of that day, all three people had declined the offer to go to Paris with her. She breathed easier then and on the way home, she planned her day. After her early morning examination, she would catch the train at 9:30 and arrive in Paris at 3:30. Where she planned to shop was irrelevant. Going by herself meant she had twelve hours by herself—six there, six back—to think. And that was exactly what she needed.

With all but one exam finished, she headed home. Angelika would try her best not to have to lie to Dieter, so she hoped he wouldn't ask her straight out who was going with her. But she would do what she had to do to make this trip by herself tomorrow. She needed time to think and come back to herself. Oh, did she ever need to think.

A few months ago she was a happily married woman. Now what was she? Certainly not happily married. Was she even happy? Definitely not. Not with another man like Rolf hanging over her head. And not just hanging over her head—she thought she was *in love* with him. Imagine! The thought made her wince. How could she have let this happen? Shaking her head, she realized that she didn't *let* it happen. It just happened. Rolf was a scary—but handsome—Nazi officer who ambled into her life and changed everything. It wasn't like she had asked for this to happen. It wasn't even like she *wanted* it to happen. She had been perfectly fine before she ever met him.

And now? Now her life was a miserable mess. What could she do about it? There was no way to stay away from him. He arrived at the house almost every weekend like he owned the place. Now he even walked in the front door without knocking. Where could she go to avoid him? She couldn't disappear every weekend, even if she had somewhere to go. It was impracticable to avoid him. Unfortunately, her feelings were growing stronger every time she saw him. Feelings that were getting impossible to ignore. The whole situation was impossible.

To make it worse, Rolf was feeling that way too, or he wouldn't have touched her like that. Why did he ever have to *touch* her? That made everything so much worse. Still at night, after Dieter was asleep and before she had dozed off, she would think about that moment and re- member how his hand felt on her cheek. How was a woman supposed to forget something like that?

But there was something she could *never* forget. She was Jewish. And Rolf was a Nazi. What would he think of her if he knew the truth? What would he *do* to her if he knew the truth? What would he do to *Dieter*—his own brother—if he found out he had married a Jew? She and Dieter could both end up in a death camp. Her life was definitely right now in the present moment.

CHAPTER THIRTY-TWO

IT was finally the weekend again. After a pleasant hike in the morning with Lady, Angela had wanted to work in the garden after lunch, but it started raining, which thwarted that idea. Dean had already planted himself in front of the television watching football. She scowled and turned away from the living room. If she closed the door and blocked the vents in the bedroom, she could get it quiet enough in there that she could read.

That's all Dean ever did was watch sports on television. There was a time when she'd watch football with him—during their courtship and when they were first married. She was embarrassed to admit that she knew all the quarterbacks and all the receivers on almost every team. She had cheered and booed and yelled at the referees like a true sports fan. Then at some point, she realized that she had to step back and evaluate whether or not that was what she really wanted.

Was she watching football because she actually wanted to, or because it was something she could share with

119

Dean? It wasn't hard to figure out. In the past, she had always hated football and wondered how that kind of nonsense could entertain anyone. So when their team had won the Super Bowl, and her favorite quarterback had retired, she was done. No regrets, and she relished her newfound extra time on Sundays, Monday nights, and any other time a game might be on television.

Easing herself into the chair, she propped the book on her lap without opening it. She was comfortable in this house, in her relationship with Dean. It wasn't necessarily a good relationship—it had ceased being that a long time ago—but it was comfortable. They knew each other, their weaknesses and strengths, all their flaws, and their likes and dislikes. But was that enough? Could she live forever like this—somewhere between happy and miserable? Was that really living?

Her thoughts drifted to everything that had gone on in their marriage since the beginning. It hadn't always been "just comfortable." It had started out good. They talked, both of them, give and take, both talking and both listening. When had it become Dean doing all the talking and she doing all the listening? How did that even happen? Then she remembered back to the beginning and realized again that she had remembered it wrong.

Dean had talked so much in the beginning that the only way for her to say anything was to interrupt. There had never been a pause with him. He would go from talking about the score of the latest game to Lady's health to his last conversation with his parents without so much as a second between topics.

Angela remembered that she had gotten so used to interrupting to get herself heard that she began to interrupt other people while they were talking—whether they talked nonstop like Dean or not. And that, she realized now, was when it stopped being a conversation with Dean. She had been so horrified at how rude she was to other people by interrupting, that to break the habit, she had to stop interrupting Dean as well. And if you didn't interrupt Dean, then you didn't say anything. It was as simple as that.

Angela took a deep breath and felt like she had just had a revelation. So that's when it began. Almost the very beginning. She had no idea. Unconsciously forming her mouth in a hard line and shaking her head, she realized that he had done all the talking and she all the listening *for years*. Her memories of them having a back and forth conversation had been distorted with time. It wasn't that way at all. Putting her book down, she went to get a snack.

As she walked by Dean in the living room, she noticed the beer in his hand. She grabbed a bag of chips and a soda from the refrigerator and then as an afterthought, she checked the recycle bin. There was already an empty can of beer in there. He was on his second beer and not even an hour into the game yet. Angela hated that. She couldn't call him a drunk, because Sunday was generally the only day he drank. But he drank so much! In the winter before they moved, when their wood stove was going, she was afraid that he would leave the door open or catch himself on fire. It was always a worry. Shaking her head, she returned to the bedroom.

Conversations. Sitting back in the chair and opening the bag of chips, she thought back to the beginning and their lack of mutual conversations. But it reminded her of something else.

When they had first started going together, she had

brought a movie to his house that they could watch together. It was an old favorite of hers called *The Conversation* starring Gene Hackman. She had seen it years earlier, thought it was wonderful, and naturally wanted to share it with Dean. But although it was a thriller, it was not an action thriller with car chases and shootings every minute. It was more of a thinking-thriller. Dean hated it. Angela should have known then how very different the two of them were. Him: sports and action and violence. Her: thinking and mutual conversations.

She sighed and picked up her book. I bet Dr. Weiss doesn't watch football, she thought.

CHAPTER THIRTY-THREE

SUNDAY morning, Dr. Weiss woke up with the sun, got dressed, and hurried downstairs. It surprised him to find Carla sitting at the kitchen table drinking coffee. "What are you doing up so early, sweetheart?" Bending over to kiss her on top of her head, he gave her shoulder an affectionate squeeze and turned to the coffee. He poured himself some coffee and sat down at the table with her.

"I'm going to a game." She took another slow sip of coffee.

Dr. Weiss chuckled. "I *know* you're not going to play!" He nodded toward the cast on her foot.

"No, Dad, I'm not going to play." She laughed and smiled at him.

"Do you need a ride, sweetie?"

Before she could answer, the dog door swished open and Wolf came bounding in, wagging his tail. "Hi, Wolfie!" She grabbed him by the scruff and pushed her face into his. When she brought her head up, she said, "No, Dad, I have a ride, thanks." When she heard a soft,

123

quick honk outside, she stood up. "There it is now." Bending over, she gave him a kiss on the forehead and limped toward the door. "Bye, Dad. Bye, Wolfie." The big dog followed her to the door and then returned to Dr. Weiss, putting his head on his knee.

Dr. Weiss finished his coffee, hugged the dog, and walked out to his car. After stopping to buy a Sunday paper, he drove to the clinic and spent most of the morning there checking on the animals and reading his various professional journals. As he returned to the house, the rain came pouring down in big, sloppy drops.

He settled onto the couch, kicked off his shoes, patted the big dog by his side, picked up the remote control and flicked on the game. Although he had intended to work in the garden, the rain had put the kibosh on that. Now all he wanted was to relax a little in front of the TV with mind-numbing entertainment. Taking a deep breath, his eyes remained unfocused on the commercial. Uneasy, he looked around and sighed. It had been so long since he had felt comfortable in his own home. What a horrible way to live. It was like he was walking on eggshells all the time, never knowing when Helen would pop up and scream at him again.

As if on cue, Helen appeared in the doorway of the den. Aside from a faint reflection on the TV screen he might not have known she was there. But he still would have *known* she was there, because he could *feel* her there. Her anger, her resentment, and her bitterness emanated from her viciously just as peace and good will had emanated from Mother Teresa *compassionately*.

Dr. Weiss remembered when he had been privileged to hear Mother Teresa speak when he was in high school. He had won a trip to Washington, D.C., after writing an essay in his social studies class. He and another student had been invited to go to the National Prayer Breakfast in 1994. That moment would always remain in his mind. A peace descended on the audience like a blanket. It was like she had cast a spell of peacefulness over all of them.

A stamp of Helen's foot brought him back to the moment. Without turning around, he knew what stance she was in: hands on hips and a frown on her face.

"You lazy good-for-nothing! Why aren't you outside working on your beloved garden? Can't you find anything more productive to do than watching that junk?"

"It's raining outside," he said quietly, staring straight ahead at the TV.

"That's no excuse! You lazy—"

Carla's words from the hospital flashed in his mind. Dr. Weiss stood up and turned toward the doorway. "I am *not* a good-for-nothing. I am *not* lazy. I have supported you and the children all these years, in the manner to which you have grown accustomed. You have never had to work a day since we've been married." He raised his voice. "So don't call me that!" Then he turned and sat back down on the couch. The dog beside him whined.

Helen, stunned that he had stood up for himself, kept silent but didn't move from the doorway. He could still *feel* her there.

At last she spoke, almost in a whisper. "I've just made a decision, Ralph. I'm going to get a job. I'm starting to look tomorrow." Then she turned and walked out.

Now it was Dr. Weiss's turn to feel stunned. He had never kept her from working and had no feelings for it or against it. It had always been her choice to stay home with the children. But the children had needed no one to

125

stay home with them for years, so Helen had filled in her time with charity and volunteer work. The rest of the time, she spent at home growing more bitter. He thought looking for a job could only be a good thing. It would be good for her, and maybe even it would be good for *them* —as a couple.

CHAPTER THIRTY-FOUR

The previous evening had gone well. Dieter never asked Angelika one question about her trip. He had talked throughout dinner *and* after dinner telling her of a complex case he had just won. After he had elaborated on every little nuance of everything he had done in the courtroom, they had gone to sleep. Early in the morning, she had left the house before he awakened, so no questions were asked. Here on the train, she didn't have to worry any more about his questions. She could just sit there on the chugging train heading toward Paris and watch the scenery go by.

Now that she had all the time in the world—nearly seven hours—to think about her life, she found that she didn't want to. She didn't want to confront those feelings that were complicating her life. Since she had all that time, she decided that she could put it off a little longer, so she picked up the book by Jung that Rolf had given her.

Angelika just held it in her hands, looking at it, turning

it over, feeling the rough cover beneath her fingers, and thinking that Rolf not only picked up the book just for her, but he had read it. His hands had been on this very cover. His fingers turned these very pages that she was about to turn. Did he think about her as he read it? Oh, probably not she mused, men can't think of more than one thing at a time! Smiling to herself at that thought, she took in a deep breath and opened the book. As she flipped through the beginning pages, some writing on the title page caught her eye. *To Angelika, A woman whose mind is as beautiful as the rest of her. Rolf.*

She slammed the book closed. When her heart started beating wildly, she put both hands over it. It felt like it would beat right out of her chest. Gazing out the window and looking at the scenery passing by, she tried to calm herself. Then she picked up the book gingerly and carefully turned the pages until she got to the title page again. The writing was still there. Somehow she thought that maybe if she turned back to it, it would have disappeared—like she had imagined it. But she hadn't. There it was in front of her for all the world to see.

Why had Rolf put it there? What if Dieter had seen it? Rolf probably put it on the title page instead of inside the front cover naively thinking that Dieter might pick it up, but he wouldn't get as far as the title page. She shrugged. It was a naive assumption, but he was probably right. Dieter wasn't any more interested in her psychology books than she was in his law books. Besides, at least Rolf didn't sign it *love* or anything. This was innocent, wasn't it? He had called her beautiful, and there was nothing wrong with that. Dieter often told her she was beautiful, so he wouldn't feel upset about his brother noticing that, too, would he? How would Dieter feel if he knew his brother had touched her cheek like that though? What if he had seen that? She shivered.

It made her realize that she did not want to lose Dieter. Or did she? Angelika's whole body sagged as she sighed and gazed out the window. This was exactly why she didn't want to think about her life. The confusion that engulfed her felt oppressive. But she knew one thing: when Dieter touched her face it felt nothing like when Rolf touched her face. Was it just someone new and exciting? Just infatuation? She didn't think so. It felt deeper than that. It felt like a heart connection.

Although she tried reading the book that was still in her lap, every time she turned to another chapter thinking maybe *that* one would keep her interest, Rolf's and Dieter's faces kept appearing on the pages before her. They revolved around her mind like they were on a merry-go-round, always shifting, first one, then the other. Whom did she really love? The question confused her. Everything confused her.

When at last the train pulled into the station in Paris, Angelika was grateful for the respite from thinking. The time alone hadn't cleared her head so she could think about the two men without emotion—if anything, it had made it worse. Now she could busy herself with shopping and sightseeing for a day or two. She hadn't decided yet how long she wanted to stay in Paris. Gathering her one bag from the train and slinging it over her shoulder —she had packed light, so she could make some purchases and still fit them in—she walked toward her destination: an outdoor cafe she and Dieter had gone to on their honeymoon. Angelika felt she needed some place to unwind from the chugging of the train and her conflicted thoughts.

As she headed there, trying not to think of anything more emotional than where she would like to shop, the sirens started. At first, she didn't understand what they were. But when all the people on the street started running, and an older woman grabbed her by the arm to pull her into the safety of a building, she realized what the sirens were: air raid sirens.

CHAPTER THIRTY-FIVE

THE two weeks between appointments were uneventful. Dean continued to annoy her with his constant complaints and even more constant talking. Lady seemed to be doing better, and her thoughts returned more often than she liked to Dr. Weiss. Now she was on her way to see him again. She wondered when the thrill that she got from seeing and talking to him would wear off. Because she knew what she *thought* she felt for him was just infatuation, nothing more.

Angela parked the car in the crowded lot, grabbed Lady's leash, and walked her into the clinic. After checking in at the desk, she sat down at the other side of the room between two hissing cats in a carrier and a tired old fox terrier sleeping in an old woman's lap. Lady lay down at Angela's feet, ignoring the cats and the dog. "You're a good girl, Lady, you know that, doncha?" Lady just looked at her and grinned, which made Angela smile. There was something about the grin of a big, powerful Rottweiler that disarmed her. Especially this

131

Rottweiler, whom Angela loved very much.

She told Lady to stay and walked to the magazine rack to pick up something to read. It looked like she'd be waiting for a while. The door opened and a puppy pulled his young owner inside. As the puppy struggled against the leash, the young boy just stood there, waiting for his parent. The puppy pulled himself out of the collar and ran around the office greeting each dog and scaring each cat he approached. Angela glanced over and saw that Lady was still where she had left her, interested in the puppy, but still unmoving. Cats in the room were hissing and scared, and dogs in the room were barking and straining at their leashes. Lady lay there, looking around at the chaos but continuing to obey the stay command.

When the parent walked in and saw the chaos in the puppy's wake, she scooped him up in her arms, apologized, and slipped the collar back around his neck. Then she proceeded to check in at the desk. Angela smiled, took two magazines to read, and sat back down. Leaning over, she petted Lady's shiny, black coat. "What a good girl you are, Lady! You were awesome!" The dog looked up and grinned.

"That's a great dog, you got there," said the woman with the fox terrier. "She never moved an inch. Even Scratchy got excited with that puppy running around." She looked down and petted her dog.

"Yeah, she's a pretty good girl, all right." Angela opened the *Audubon* magazine she had picked up and began reading. She didn't want to get into a protracted conversation with the woman.

The tech called the woman into the examining room next, so it didn't matter. Thirty minutes later, after Angela had finished the *Audubon* magazine and was halfway through *People*, most of the animals that were in the waiting room when she had arrived had left. A whole new crop of dogs, cats, and their owners now filled the room. The only one who remained from the initial group was the woman with the two cats who sat next to her. But neither she nor the other woman made any effort to move. Both cats had stopped hissing and were at the edge of the cage, one trying to whack Lady with a paw stuck through the cage door. Lady, just out of reach, looked at the two cats, smiled, and kept smiling until it was the woman's turn to leave.

The woman with the cats walked out of the examining room at last. A few minutes later, Dr. Weiss stood there scanning the waiting room for Angela and Lady. When he saw them, he smiled, and motioned them in.

"Hello, Angie," he said without looking at the chart. He patted Lady on the head. "Hi, Lady, how are you doing today?" He kneeled down to look at her eye. She looked up at him and wagged her stub of a tail. While still examining her eyes, he said, "How's she been? Any changes? Rubbing her eye? You still giving her the drops every day?" When he finished looking at the eye, he stood up and faced her.

"She's been great. Active, happy. Nothing changed that I noticed, and no rubbing of her eye. And yes, of course I'm giving her the drops every day."

Dr. Weiss chuckled. "Just asking. Not everybody does."

"Well, I do." Angie smiled at him and again noticed how good he looked with the shaggy hair.

"Okay, good." He placed Lady's chart on the examining table and scribbled notes on it.

When he looked up again, Angela smiled at him. "So I cooked grass-fed hamburgers last night with baked sweet potato fries. What did you cook?"

"Oh, I don't cook." He glanced at Lady.

"Okay, then. What did you eat?"

"Lean beef, broccoli, salad."

"Sounds good. But I bet your dog doesn't eat that well."

He laughed. "Wolf eats very well. But probably not the same as Lady, because his owner doesn't believe the same things."

Angela shivered for some reason when she heard the dog's name, but she didn't know why and tried to hide it. "Yes, I know you're right, Dr. Weiss!" Not knowing why she even did it, she asked, "Do you meditate? It's good for you—and as important as good food."

Dr. Weiss did a strange thing, then. He looked behind him, then turned the other way and looked again, straining his neck to check around the corner. Then he leaned across the examining table and said in a low voice just above a whisper, "This is where I get my peace."

He said it with such gravity that she didn't know how to respond, so she stepped back and just looked at him.

Dr. Weiss nodded, as if to himself, then picked up Lady's chart, stepped to the doorway, and turned around to look at her. "Look, I'd love to stand here and talk with you, but the waiting room is full, and I've been behind all day. I need to see Lady again in a month." He patted Lady on the head. "Bye, Angie."

"Bye, Dr. Weiss." She wasn't sure he heard that, though, because he was already out the door.

CHAPTER THIRTY-SIX

DR. Weiss stepped out of the room and turned sharply to his right. From that vantage point, he could peer back into the room, but the occupants couldn't see him unless they knew where to look. The woman, Angie, had already moved toward the door. He had no idea why he had told her that he got his peace at the clinic. It was true, but still, it wasn't something he'd normally share with a client. He didn't know her well—he barely knew her at all—and yet he felt an unusual connection as if he had known her his whole life. Taking a deep breath, he started toward the other examining room where he was sure the next patient was waiting.

He thought about how busy he was and how well he had provided for his family through the years. And he wondered why Helen would want to get a job now. The kids had been teenagers for years, and she had never shown any inclination to want a job before this. It was curious. And he didn't have time to think about his disclosure to Angie or about Helen's decision to get a job any more until the end of the day when he could relax again in his office.

It had been a long day of seeing patients. He loved the patients—who wouldn't love the cuddly dogs and cats and the occasional bearded dragon—but it was their owners he sometimes had problems with. The bad ones insisted they had done nothing wrong, when it was obvious they had, and then some of them neglected to give their pets medication as required. They said they loved their pets, but didn't show it. Dr. Weiss preferred the days he did surgery in the morning and only saw patients in the afternoon. That was much more pleasant for him. If all the owners were like Angie, he wouldn't mind seeing patients every day. He shrugged, smiled, and turned to his computer.

The only email he had received was from his daughter, Carla: *Daddy, just wanted to tell you how much I love you!* How fortunate he was to have good children. Carla and Curtis had both slipped away as they got older and started new activities on their own. But they were good kids, and he was grateful that he'd had no problems with either of them. Carla breaking her ankle was the worst thing that had ever happened to either her or Curtis. Dr. Weiss knocked on his wooden desk which made him smile. He was a scientific man, but it didn't hurt to be careful.

He turned off the computer and sat in his easy chair. Now, at last, he could reflect on his day. It still stunned him that he had told Angie about getting his peace at the clinic. Although it was true, telling one of his clients bewildered him. It was unheard of. He still couldn't believe he had done that. What had possessed him to tell her that? Furrowing his brow and thinking back on that moment, he realized that when it happened, it had felt natural to tell her. But the way he had told her! That, he could have handled differently. The way he looked around left and right must have seemed suspicious to her. She probably thought he was going to confess to using drugs!

All at once he was both embarrassed and not embarrassed. Although she had stepped back in confusion at his intensity, he still thought she understood—or perhaps would understand. Dr. Weiss felt certain about that. She *understood* him. And when he thought back on his marriage—even the early days—had Helen *ever* understood him? He didn't think so. The beginning of his marriage was all rainbows and roses—like all new marriages were —full of hope and dreams. And when the familiarity set in and the passion wore off, then there were the births of the children to sustain them. That was enough for a long time. And now? Now it felt like there was nothing left between them.

He still didn't understand what Helen's motivation was to find a job, but it was fine with him. Maybe it would take the edge off her anger and bitterness. There was one thing he was sure about. If she found a job, it could only be better for both of them. Because there was no way it could get any worse.

CHAPTER THIRTY-SEVEN

ANGELA paid for her visit and hurried out to the car. She wasn't going to lean against the building again trying to recover from their conversation. That would not be something she did every time she came out of his clinic. But after sticking the key in the ignition, she didn't turn the car on, because she wanted to think about what had just happened.

Dr. Weiss had told her something personal and private. That much was clear. And looking behind himself, right and left, like he did? That made it even more extreme. It was like he was trusting her and her alone with something intimate from his personal life. It had been so intense that she had unconsciously stepped back. Now she shook her head. She shouldn't have done that. And after she *had* done that, what did he do? He immediately left. Yes, she had messed up. They didn't even get to have one of their good conversations because his intensity had overwhelmed her. Bad mistake. She shouldn't have let it get to her like that.

Starting the car and pulling out of the lot, Angela tried clearing her mind so she could concentrate and get a better picture of what had happened. Then she laughed. *What just happened*, she scoffed to herself. Nothing *happened*! She was married and this was a business meeting. She *paid* him to take care of her dog. "And a very good dog you are, Lady!" Stopped at a light, she leaned over and cuddled the dog's head in her hands.

Her mind came back to Dr. Weiss looking behind him both ways and how he had leaned forward and whispered about getting his peace at the clinic. *That* did not feel like a business meeting to her. Again she tried clearing her mind so she could be objective about everything that did or didn't happen between them.

Deciding to start with her entering the clinic, in her mind's eye she saw herself lead Lady into the clinic and then check in at the reception desk. Continuing, she saw herself sit down in the crowded waiting room. Every time the examining room opened, she had glanced up, hoping to get an early glimpse of Dr. Weiss. And every time it opened, it was a tech standing there instead of the doctor. Every time! In the thirty-five minutes she had sat in that waiting room, the only time that Dr. Weiss had come to the door to call a patient in was once—when he called her and Lady!

Taking a deep breath, she noticed how hard she was gripping the steering wheel, so she loosened her grip and exhaled sharply. There! So there was something between them. Of the two things that had happened—him calling her and only her, and leaning forward telling her a *personal secret*—the latter was more important, but the evidence was building. She wasn't imagining the connection between them.

Then she remembered something else. When Dr. Weiss mentioned his dog's name, Wolf, Angela had shivered. Thinking about it now caused her to shiver once again. Angela had heard the word wolf before a thousand times and had never had a reaction like that. And then a voice inside her said, *but you've never heard the name Wolf.* That much was true. Still, why did the name Wolf strike such an odd cord in her? Why did it make her feel like she was longing for something she couldn't have?

Moving her body trying to shake off these—almost disturbing—thoughts, she came up with something else. Something she should have done and didn't. Or rather something she should have said, but didn't. When she had asked him about what he had eaten the night before, he said he didn't cook, but he ate lean meat, broccoli, and salad. That didn't sound at all like something you could order from a restaurant. So who cooked his lean beef for him if he didn't cook it himself? That was the question she should have asked.

When he was looking into Lady's eye, she had looked again and found no wedding ring on his finger. That wasn't always reliable, though, because some men didn't wear one. Dr. Weiss didn't seem like a womanizer, so why didn't he wear a ring *if* he was married? *If* being the qualifier there. Because of the surgery he did? No rings underneath his gloved hands? Angela shrugged her shoulders. There was no way for her to know. Then she took a deep breath and nodded to herself. Yes, there was. She would have to ask him.

CHAPTER THIRTY-EIGHT

When Dr. Weiss arrived home that evening, Wolf met him at the door, wagging and smiling. Dr. Weiss kneeled down and hugged the big dog. "You're always steadfast and loyal, aren't you, big boy?" When he looked up, he saw that Carla was sitting at the kitchen table talking on her cellphone. She nodded to him, finished her conversation, and put the phone down on the table.

"Hi, Daddy. Listen, Mom didn't cook tonight, so Curt ordered pizza. There's still a few slices over there." She motioned toward the counter, then stood up, gave him a quick hug, and hobbled off, cellphone in hand.

"Carla, wait!" When she turned around, he continued. "Why didn't Mom cook? Did she say?"

"She seemed real depressed. She said she had a hard day searching for work and didn't feel like cooking. And she said we were all old enough to fend for ourselves!"

"Did she eat?"

"Not that I know of, but maybe she ate something before she got home."

141

"Okay, thanks, Carla." But he was talking to her back. Carla had already left the room.

Shrugging his shoulders, he opened the pizza box. Inside was one of his favorite pizzas: Canadian bacon and pineapple. Selecting two of the four pieces, he put them on a plate and slipped them into the microwave. The kids ate their pizza cold, but he never had a taste for it that way. While he waited for the microwave, he reached into his wallet and pulled out thirty dollars to pay for the pizza. Dr. Weiss was grateful to Curtis for getting the pizza. He didn't feel like going back out again or trying to scrounge up something to eat. Cooking never had been one of his strong suits.

Sitting down at the table with the now-hot pizza, he felt guilty about eating what he considered junk food. But he only had it on rare occasions such as this, so he pushed the guilt away and enjoyed the delectable flavors in the pizza. Soon, though, he wondered if Helen had eaten and why she felt depressed. It wasn't as if she *needed* a job. Her looking for a job was completely voluntary. And still, Dr. Weiss didn't understand why she even *wanted* a job.

It didn't matter though. Helen was free to do whatever she wanted. She always was free like that, which made Dr. Weiss wonder again for about the millionth time why she had become so angry and bitter in the last few years. He had long ago stopped trying to fix it and had just tried to endure it without becoming angry and bitter himself. What had saved him from that?

That made him think about his conversation that morning with Angie when she had asked him if he meditated. Working at the clinic, doing work he not only loved, but that mattered, was like a meditation to him.

And he felt certain that was what had kept him from becoming angry and bitter.

Thoughts of his brief time with Angie made him smile. Thoughts of her always made him smile—compared to thoughts of Helen that made him feel bad. But he pushed unpleasant thoughts of Helen aside so he could think of Angie. Although he didn't understand why he shared with her his feelings of peace at the clinic, he felt no embarrassment from it anymore. She needed to know that. Wait! Why? Why would he think that, and why would she need to know that?

He shook his head forcefully from side to side. His life was getting strange. That was for sure. Taking a slow deep breath, he again returned to the morning's conversation. She had asked about how he ate, and after he had said he didn't cook, he had told her what he usually ate. He was glad she hadn't asked him any more questions that would compel him to tell her he was married, because he didn't want to do that. *Why* he didn't was another good question, for which he didn't know the answer.

There was something else about the conversation that had struck him but now he couldn't remember what it was, so he went over their words in his head. Ah, yes. It was when he told Angie that Wolf ate very well. It had looked like she shivered at the mention of the dog's name. How curious that was. Maybe it was just that she once had a dog named Wolf. That must be it. It was all he could think of, anyway. If it was something else, it was nothing he could imagine.

143

CHAPTER THIRTY-NINE

Angelika now found herself inside a tall brick building. That's all she got to see before descending the cement staircase to the bomb shelter. Everybody was rushing, and the people behind her pushing her forward made her fear she would tumble down the stairs. But the people behind pushed her forward into the people in front of her making *her* one of the people pushing. The bodies were packed too closely together for anyone to fall.

And there was good reason to be rushing too. She could feel the impact from the bombs even before she reached the bottom of the stairs. Angelika didn't think they were close—at least she hoped not—but the vibration of them rattled her anyway. Upon reaching the bottom, most people were still standing up, milling around in what little space there was. She didn't know how many people would still come down those stairs and squeeze into the crowd, but she was very grateful she was already there.

Five minutes later, only a handful of people trickled in,

and she heard a solid door at the top of the stairs slam shut. With that sound, she let her body relax. But her feeling of safety was misleading. If a bomb made a direct hit on the building, it would crumble to the ground, killing all those who waited in the false safety of the bomb shelter. She knew as well as anyone that shelters protected you only if the bombs fell *elsewhere.*

Standing in the dim light of a bare bulb above her, she clung to her bag as though it were a lifeline. When people began to sit down on the edges of the big room, she felt grateful that she found a place with a cushion. But even sitting on the cold floor would have been welcome. Waiting for the bombs to stop while standing up seemed much more difficult than waiting for the bombs to stop sitting down. And she wondered how long she would have to wait for the bombs to stop.

This was the first time that Paris was bombed, she knew that. Other cities like Dunkirk and Boulogne had recently been bombed—she had heard at school—but not Paris. If she had ever imagined it would happen, she would never have come here. Hindsight, she thought, as another bomb vibrated the walls of the building. Her thoughts were interrupted by the shaking of the woman next to her. When Angelika turned to her, she realized that the woman cried in big pulsing sobs. She put her arm around the woman and tried to comfort her.

The woman hiccupped out a few words. "I'm safe, but my children—my children are at school, and I've heard the Germans like to bomb schools to demoralize the people. I'm so frightened for my children." Angelika just held the woman until she eventually stopped sobbing. When she heard the woman softly snoring, Angelika removed her arm.

As she sat there looking around and still gripping her bag, Angelika thought about her life back in Germany—her confusion about the two men in her life. And she realized that she had not thought of either of them since the bombing started. She had thought it was so important to get away and figure out her life, and now here she sat in a bomb shelter, while her own people bombed the city. Her life was at risk, and her problems with Rolf and Dieter seemed non-essential when she realized that. When your life is on the line, nothing else matters. Angelika was certain of that.

More than two hours later—although it seemed much longer than that—it registered in her brain that she hadn't felt the reverberation of the bombs in quite some time. People were starting to stand up. When she saw that some of them were heading up the stairs, she gently shook the sleeping woman next to her until her eyes opened with a shocked expression. Then the woman nodded her head resolutely and stood. Angelika made her way to the stairs and drifted up them in the same crowded way as she had descended them. Wall to wall bodies gratefully all moving in the same direction.

At the top of the stairs, the crowd continued moving until they emerged from the building into the not so bright light of day. Smoke drifted heavily through the air, some places denser than others. Although no bombs had fallen close to the brick building, she could see wreckage down the street which made her shiver. There were fires burning in the distance. She could see the lick of the orange flames through the smoke. The steady tone of the "all-clear" siren was sounding, which she hadn't heard from the basement of the building. Police cars crawled down the streets surveying the damage. Later, she knew they would search for the wounded—and the dead.

Standing against the building and looking around, she suddenly realized that she needed to leave as soon as she could. The Germans could come back at any time and start bombing again. Funny, she thought. "The Germans." They were not *her* people. These were Hitler's people, not hers. Did she even consider herself German anymore? Taking a deep breath, she forced herself to move toward the train station. She had to force herself because what she really wanted to do was sit down where she was and have a good cry. And that would never do.

Would the train station even still be there? Gratefully, it was. She didn't know how long it would be until the next train would leave, but she intended to be on it. There were ten frightened people in front of her in line, and as she stood there, the line behind her grew longer and longer each passing minute. When it was her turn, she stepped up to the window and asked the clerk in German when the next train would be. It was only the clerk's wide-eyed stare that made her realize what she had done. Since she arrived, she had only spoken French, so she didn't know why she had suddenly reverted to her native language. When she repeated the question in French, the clerk said, "There will be no trains going to Germany any time soon. Why would you even *want* to go there?"

Angelika shrugged her shoulders and said, "My husband is there." When the clerk looked up in alarm, Angelika added, "He's *not* a Nazi."

The clerk shook his head. "The closest I can get you is Geneva, Switzerland. You're on your own from there. But I'd think twice about returning to Germany right now."

Angelika nodded and purchased a ticket to Geneva. "How soon does it leave?"

"You're in luck! It leaves in fifteen minutes. You just made it! Go that way. You'll see the sign."

Angelika thanked the clerk and headed the direction that the clerk had indicated. They were already boarding when she reached the sign, and as she stepped into the train, she bid Paris a not-so-fond farewell. Not long after, sitting in her seat in the crowded train—every seat was filled and people standing in the aisles still looking for one—she tried to relax as the train pulled out of the station.

After a few minutes of the train chugging along, and after she stopped shaking from the bombing nightmare, she felt relaxed enough to think clearly again—about the two men in her life. But as she hugged her bag to herself, all she could think of was who she would want to comfort her right now after her fearful experiences in Paris. Whose arms would she want around her right now? Her steadfast husband, Dieter? Or the handsome Nazi—yes, Nazi—officer Rolf? Dieter was always there for her. But Rolf talked to her about things that were important to her. Dieter was always there, but Rolf gave her butterflies. Right now? She would want Rolf's arms around her. Yes. Rolf.

CHAPTER FORTY

ALL the way home Angela replayed the entire visit in her head again and again. She thought Lady would tire of hearing her talking to herself about the situation, but Lady sat there, looking out the window and smiling back at her when addressed. What if I had said this, thought Angela. What if I hadn't said that? The speculations and self-recriminations of not doing or saying the right thing continued until she pulled up in front of the old farmhouse.

Walking Lady out back to play, she undid the leash from her collar and let her run. Lady found an old ball in the field and brought it back. After fifteen minutes of playing, Lady lay down at her feet, panting. "Okay, sweet girl, let's go inside. You've had a big day, haven't you?" She hugged Lady and walked her into the house.

On the drive into work after the appointment, and the drive home from work that afternoon, she replayed everything in her mind again. Luckily, she was busy enough at work that she didn't have one extra minute to

149

give it a thought. When she parked again in front of the house, she realized how stupid she had been for spending all that time on five minutes of her life. That's all that she was with him: five minutes. And she had blown that five minutes completely out of proportion.

Laughing at herself, she sank down on the couch and picked up the remote control. When the television flicked on, it came on to one of Dean's sports stations. Angela couldn't get the station changed quickly enough. She hated that! It was so stupid being angry at something so minor, and yet it seemed like it was a reflection of their entire relationship. She *hated* sports. And Dean loved them. Even after changing the station, it was all Angela could do to keep herself from throwing the remote across the room. Instead of trying to fight it, she flicked off the television, stuffed the remote beside the couch cushion just to be mean, and walked to the bedroom to read.

She had been reading for fifteen minutes when the blinking light of the answering machine caught her eye. Since both she and Dean had cell phones, they rarely used and even more rarely received calls on the landline. Standing up and taking the two steps to the device, she pushed the button. It was Dean. Why hadn't he called her cell, she wondered in the seconds it took for him to say his name. "Hi, honey. Listen, I'll be staying late tonight. Have good news! See you soon!"

Good news was good, she thought. Usually Dean came home and complained about his job. Since he had gone full time, though, he seemed to be better. Although how he could feel excited about being a file clerk, she didn't know. And if she was honest, she thought he was justified in complaining about *this particular job*. Trouble was, complaining about his job was something he had done so often in the years they had been together, that she hated hearing it, regardless of it being justified. Looking at the clock, she nodded her head and then returned to her book.

Forty-five minutes later, she had heard nothing from Dean and wondered just how late he would be. It would take him thirty minutes to drive home, and since the time function didn't work on their answering machine, she didn't know what time he had called. She walked into the front room and looked out the window. How long would he be? She didn't like this kind of uncertainty and wished that he had said how late he would be. Should she worry that he wasn't home yet, or more to the point, *when* should she worry that he wasn't home yet?

Remembering back to her dating days when she only liked *bad boys*, she thought about how many times she had waited by the phone—or a window—for someone who either never called or never showed up, or did so hours after expected. Angela knew one thing. She didn't want to go through that again.

That made her think about Dr. Weiss. Was he the kind of man who would do that to a woman? No, she didn't think he was. He seemed responsible and reliable—at least he seemed that way in what little she knew about him, which in reality, was very little. Maybe he was a drunk and a wife beater, she had no way to know. And that thought brought her back around to the question she had been wondering about all day: was he married or not?

CHAPTER FORTY-ONE

THE following evening when Dr. Weiss returned home, he found another pizza waiting for him on the counter, pepperoni and mushroom. Frowning and sighing, he put two slices into the microwave and pulled out more money from his wallet. It was good of Curtis to do that, but when would Helen start cooking again? Although it had only been two days, he didn't intend to eat this way for very long.

He sat down at the table to eat the pizza. But this time he wasn't able to push away the guilt as easily as he had done the day before. It tasted good, though, so he thought he might as well enjoy it. Once Helen got back to her old self, he would have good dinners to come home to again.

As he sat there steaming about the lack of a healthy and nutritious dinner, he stuffed the pizza in his mouth and chomped on it, nodding his head and getting angrier and angrier. Suddenly, he burst out laughing. He laughed so hard that he had to put the pizza down and push his chair away from the table.

Imagine, he thought to himself, thinking Helen *owed* him a good dinner. She didn't *owe* him anything. Their relationship of the last few years had been her cooking him dinner and cleaning the house, and him bringing home the money. That was it. No talking, no nothing. Cooking/cleaning/money. What a sad state of affairs that was. As he ate, he realized that he mourned the loss of their relationship more than he mourned the loss of a good meal.

Dr. Weiss wasn't sure where they had gone wrong, but gone wrong they had, and he suspected it was too late to fix anything now. He had tried. He felt strongly about that; he *had* tried. Still, he had no intention of leaving the relationship—no matter how bad it got—and damaging the children. What would a divorce *do* to them? It was unthinkable. No, he'd never do that.

Thinking of the children made him think once again what Carla had said to him when she was in the hospital: "Why do you let her treat you like that?" He wondered if that could have been the drugs talking. When he had stood up to Helen the other day, was that what had driven her to want to get a job? Had he done the wrong thing? Should he apologize?

He put his head in his hands and sighed. Then he pushed himself away from the table without finishing. This kind of thinking would get him nowhere. When he thought about apologizing to Helen for standing up to her, it gave him a bad feeling in his stomach. That didn't feel like the right thing to do. She had been yelling and berating him for years without him doing a thing about it. She should apologize to him. Carla may have said that under the influence of the drugs, but he bet she had been thinking it for a while. It was only that the drugs had given her the courage to say something like that in front of her mother.

Dr. Weiss had no reason to feel bad about standing up for himself. Come to think of it, why hadn't he stood up for himself before that? Nobody deserved to be treated that way, and in reality, he had *allowed* it for years. She may have her reasons for treating him badly, but he had done nothing overtly to hurt her. He had never been unfaithful, never come home drunk, never gambled. He was a good man! And then he thought for several more minutes about what a good man he was.

But he had to admit that while he had done none of those things, there were things he had done that were probably why Helen had come to hate him so. He was often late for dinner if an animal needed his attention, he had been late or even no-show at some of their dinner parties because an animal had needed him, and even while they were out to dinner he would sometimes get an emergency call at the clinic and would have to leave her there all alone. But the animals! How could he not be there when they needed him? He *had* to be. And he had always called. There was not a single time when she hadn't known where he was.

It was what he had chosen in his life, and Helen should have known that. She wanted a "regular" husband who was home with her all the time. Dr. Weiss was never that man. He hadn't been that man when they were dating, and he had never told her that he was that kind of man, nor had he ever pretended to be that kind of man. Dr. Weiss had never deceived her.

It was all a matter of expectations. She expected him to be that kind of man. And he expected her to understand the kind of man that he was.

CHAPTER FORTY-TWO

ANGELA still felt furious. She sat in her office in front of her computer with no one else in the entire building. Because she wanted to get out of the house before Dean got up, she had left early and had sat here deleting old emails and trying not to let her anger boil over.

Dean hadn't come home until eleven o'clock the previous night. Although she had been reading in the bedroom when he drove up, she had flicked out the light right away and climbed into bed. When he stumbled into the bedroom, reeking of alcohol, he had leaned over the bed and put too much weight on her arm as he tried to whisper in her ear. Although she grimaced, she didn't think that he could see her face in the dark.

"I know you're awake, and you're probably mad, but I got promoted! And a raise! Isn't that reason enough to go out and celebrate?" It wasn't a whisper though. If she had been asleep, he would have woken her. He spoke so loudly that she could have heard him in the next room. "It's okay, though. We'll talk tomorrow." His slurred

156

speech made her wonder how he drove home.

When she had left the house that morning, she saw how he had parked in their driveway: crooked. He had parked so close to her left rear bumper that she couldn't even walk between the cars. Luckily, he didn't break her tail light. As she moved his car so she could back hers out of the driveway, her fury built. On the way to work, she had hit her dashboard so many times, it surprised her that she hadn't dented it.

And then, long before anyone else had arrived at the office, her phone had rung three times. Angela knew it was Dean although he hadn't left a message, because no one else would call this early. The fourth time it rang, he had left a message. "Angela." His curt voice sounded as if he was angry with her. "I don't know if you remember last night or not." Dude! She thought. I'm not the one who came home drunk. "I got promoted and got a raise. Now we can look for a house. I'll talk to you when I get home tonight. Bye." He hung up without even saying *I love you*. Fine, thought Angela. You drunk jerk!

And then Angela remembered. It wasn't just the bad boys who hadn't called or shown up when expected. Shortly after they were married, Dean had done the same thing. And then come home drunk. When they were still going together, he would have his nights out with the boys, but he had always called when he got home, slurring his words, but sincere. At the time, she had thought it was sweet.

But after they were married, if she received a phone call at all, it was a brief one not even saying when he'd be home—like last night's call. She remembered one time when she had grown tired of waiting for him. So she marched her little butt down to the bar she knew he frequented and bodily pulled him out and put him in the car. And it wasn't an easy task, either. He was so drunk he could barely walk, and she had to hold him up. The drunk times stopped after that. It may have helped that she had screamed at him and threatened a divorce if he didn't leave his drinking days behind.

She shook her head at the memory of it all. Last night's "event" had brought it all back in technicolor. Bad memories she never wanted to relive again. Was it starting again, she wondered. If so, she knew just what she'd do: leave. That made her wonder if she was just looking for an excuse to leave. No, but maybe she needed one. While Angela did love Dean, she wasn't sure if she was still *in love* with him—whatever that meant.

Glancing at the clock, she saw that she had less than an hour of silence before people started shuffling into the building. She took her hand off her mouse and allowed herself to think about Dr. Weiss again. Angela wondered if he always called his wife when he was late. Wife? What was she thinking? She still hadn't found out if he was married or not. That was now her prime focus. Making a promise to herself, she would not leave that clinic next month until she knew for sure if he was married or not.

Thinking back to her early days in college, she remembered the kind of man she preferred dating. It wasn't the doctor or lawyer type, it was more likely the guy painting the dorm walls. Because there was one thing that Angela was always clear about. She preferred her nights spent with the man she loved, not waiting for that man to arrive home. And Angela was aware of the hours of a doctor—any professional man. They were slaves to their profession—which was generally their passion. And she had wanted none of that. She had wanted to have her man home with her at night, to enjoy his company.

That backfired, didn't it, she thought. Excepting last night, Dean was home with her every night, and she had wished he wasn't. He never stopped talking, rarely listened, and if the television programs didn't consist of sports or a car chase, he wasn't interested. Laughing to herself, she glanced at the clock as it moved toward the time people would arrive. Angela frowned and put her hand back on her mouse. A doctor sounded pretty good to her.

CHAPTER FORTY-THREE

AFTER another long wonderful day at the clinic, Dr. Weiss sat down at his computer to check his email. Nothing. Not even one email. It didn't bother him though. He wasn't a slave to technology and didn't use the thing often anyway. Carla's occasional emails were about all he ever received. After turning off the computer, instead of sitting in the chair to read his medical journals, he decided that he'd stop for Chinese on the way home and surprise Helen. He'd get her egg foo young—her old favorite. That should please her whether she had been successful at finding a job or not. He punched the number to their house. No one answered, so he left a message on voicemail.

"Helen? If you haven't started dinner yet, don't. I'm bringing Chinese food home! Your favorite! Bye! Love you!"

When he got home, before he entered the house, the sky drew his attention. The sun had just set and the eastern sky displayed a mix of pale pink and pale blue.

Beautiful. He walked into the house, and Wolf greeted him, as usual. "How's my big boy?" Dr. Weiss patted him on the head and put the food on the table with a smile on his face. Maybe this would put him back into Helen's good graces.

Then she appeared at the door. "Late as usual!" She huffed.

He was confused, not only by her attitude, but her statement. "But I came home right after my last patient. I'm early."

She glowered at him and took her time shaking her head from side to side. Then she pointed to the clock on the wall above the sink, turned, and stomped out of the room.

It shocked Dr. Weiss when he looked at the clock and saw it was already seven o'clock. He had no idea. Still, he ran after her.

"Helen! Helen!"

Helen turned around and glowered at him again. "What do *you* want?"

"Helen, maybe you should give up on getting a job. You've been perfectly happy not working for all these years. Why change that now?"

"*What* makes you think I've been perfectly happy all these years? That's exactly what's wrong with you, Ralph. You have no idea what makes me happy." Then she turned and marched up the stairs.

Walking back into the kitchen, he slumped into the chair in front of the Chinese food. He thought he had given her everything she wanted: a nice home, plenty of money, two wonderful children. But there was still that other expectation he couldn't give her. His undivided time and attention.

The clinic was more than where he got his peace. It was also his passion. His passion was for healing. Healing animals. She had known that. Didn't she? How could she not have known that? She wanted him to be something that he could never be. And that was the one thing he couldn't give her.

Wolf came over and nuzzled him, so he leaned down and hugged the big head. "You always love me no matter how late I am, don't you, Wolfie?" The big dog licked his chin. Dr. Weiss stood up, grabbed a plate and silverware, sat back down, and served himself some Chinese food.

Since he couldn't give Helen the one thing she wanted, and what he could give her, she didn't want, maybe it was time to stop trying. Dr. Weiss shrugged. He could only do what he could do. And giving up the clinic was out of the question.

As he ate, he decided that not only had she beaten him up enough, but he had beaten himself up enough. Time to let it go. Let whatever might happen, happen. He was incapable of doing anything about it. And he knew he had tried his best. Exhaling slowly, he made up his mind. From this moment on, he would not make any more attempts to make that woman happy. It would have to be up to her. Isn't that what they said? You can only help people if they want to help themselves? Hmmm, he thought. Helen was trying to get a job, so maybe she *was* trying to help herself. Maybe she was.

Now, however, he would prefer thinking happier thoughts. Like about that woman, Angie. She was bright and happy and interesting. And she acted like she liked him. *And* she listened to him and treated him well. Then again, she had no reason not to. If only everything in his life were different, he mused. Then he could think about asking her out on a date. That made him almost choke on his mouthful of food. How long it had been since he had been on a date! Did he even want to go there? Probably not, considering where it had brought him to now. Then again, Angie was different. He just knew she was.

CHAPTER FORTY-FOUR

GERMANY/SWITZERLAND JUNE 3, 1940

Rolf was holding her. He had his arms wrapped around her from behind. She leaned into him. The train lurched, and Angelika woke up leaning against the window of the train with her arms wrapped around herself. Her bag had rolled off her lap onto the floor and against the legs of the taciturn man sitting beside her. Bending down, she pulled the bag back into her lap and hugged it to her. The cold window had made the shoulder leaning against it stiff.

It was dark outside. So black that she couldn't see anything. It must be cloudy because even the stars were missing. The only light inside the train came from the dim lights illuminating the aisle. Angelika could have turned the light on above the seat so she could read, but she chose not to.

As she looked out the window into the darkness, what had happened in Paris came back to her in moments of remembered terror. She hugged her bag tighter and closed her eyes, but the images just got more intense.

Rushing down the stairs in the stream of bodies that carried her along, sitting on a cushion on the floor watching the haunted eyes of those around her, listening to the woman next to her worried about her children, the vibrations of the bombs hitting the ground, going up the stairs again with other bodies pressed close, and then hearing the all-clear signal announcing the end of the bombing. Then she remembered standing against the building in the choking smoke and watching the panicked movements of the people all around her.

And her escape on the train. How lucky she was to have caught it, even though it was only taking her to Geneva. At least it was taking her out of Paris—her main concern. Angelika closed her eyes again and began shaking, slowly at first and then uncontrollably. It wasn't cold in the train, and at first she didn't understand what was happening. Then the images and sensations came back to her again, and she recognized it for what it was: traumatic response. Jung might call what she had gone through a psychological crisis. And what would he suggest? Perhaps discussing it with someone so she didn't repress it.

The man next to her was snoring to himself. But even if he wasn't, he didn't seem inclined to talk or listen. She looked around the train car. It was packed. But the people in it were visibly frightened and either talking among themselves, or like the man seated next to her, scared silent. So she started describing—in her mind—every second of her experience starting from the air-raid sirens when she arrived in Paris and ending with jumping onto this train hoping to get somewhere safe.

At the end of her first discourse, the shaking hadn't diminished at all, and she had started crying. At the end

165

of the second time through, the shaking had let up some, but the tears were still streaming down her face. So she repeated everything again, and when the shaking had still not completely subsided and the tears still fell, she repeated it again. And again. And again. Sometime after that, with her eyes red and her cheeks stained with teardrops, she fell asleep.

When the train slowed down for its arrival in Geneva, it woke Angelika. At first she felt disoriented, but the movement of the train brought it all back again—every painful part of it. She stood up, still holding onto her bag, and moved toward the exit. It was past midnight, and there was a coolness in the air.

Walking into the station, she looked around to see what time the train to Munich would leave. The closest she could get to Munich now would be Zurich, through Bern, and that train didn't leave for nearly three hours. After purchasing her ticket to Zurich, she slumped down in a chair to wait. The ticket agent had assured her if she waited until she arrived at Zurich to make her plans to Munich, they would have updated information that would be more accurate.

Angelika looked around the large open room. Most of the people who had shared the train with her had already dispersed. There were a handful of people in the room—a couple of them looked like they were sleeping in the chairs. But she didn't want to sleep; she didn't want to think, either. Too much of that already. So she opened her bag, pulled out the book on Jung that Rolf had given her, and started reading.

Two hours later, she had just finished the chapter on "synchronicity," when they started boarding the train. The train car was not as crowded as the train from Paris, and Angelika found herself in the same seat as when she had arrived. The tiniest feeling of familiarity made her feel more at ease as silly as that sounded and felt. But she put the bag beside her on the seat and made herself comfortable.

Five minutes before the train left the station, a woman hurried in and stood in the aisle looking at Angelika. "May I sit here, please?"

Angelika grabbed for her bag without even thinking the entire train car—probably most of the train—was empty. "Yeah, sure."

The woman plopped down next to her and tossed her bag into the seat across the aisle. Then with a big smile on her face, she stuck out her hand toward Angelika. "Hi. I'm Sigrid!"

The woman's warmth was evident, and Angelika couldn't help but smile back. She shook her hand. "Hi, Sigrid! I'm Angelika!" And she realized that was the first time she had smiled in many hours.

CHAPTER FORTY-FIVE

AT the end of the work day, Angela prepared herself to leave. She was in no hurry to get home and talk to Dean after the previous night. He had not called again during the day, and she was grateful for that. Walking out to the car, she put the key in the lock, but didn't turn it. Instead, she turned to look at everything around her. There was a lone tree in the parking lot, and in it were singing birds. She didn't know what kind, but when she got a glimpse of one of them, she saw that its head was a muted shade of red. The sky was a faded afternoon blue, and the streets were busy with traffic—little Thoreau's version of rush-hour traffic. Angela smiled, unlocked the car, and slid onto the seat.

This would be the longest drive home in the history of womankind, she thought. Angela remembered back to Dean's phone call—a part of the message she had ignored all day. He mentioned looking for a house. Shaking her head, she wasn't even sure if she wanted to *stay* with him let alone buy a house with him! What a

168

predicament. What a miserable predicament. There was no way to avoid the confrontation or conversation that awaited her when she got home. So she might as well buck up and get it over with. Deciding that, she pressed her foot down on the gas.

When she arrived home, Dean was already there. His car parked nice and straight as usual, so he hadn't been drinking before he came home from work. At least that much was good. Arguing with a drunk was a waste of energy. She took a deep breath and walked into the house like she belonged there.

Dean stood there looking more dressed up than he ever did in his job as a file clerk. Lady sat next to him. "Hello, Dean," she said with a frown on her face.

He swept his arm in front of him with a flourish. "Aren't you going to congratulate me for my promotion?"

"Congratulations!" She decided to go through the motions, so she hugged him and kissed him on the cheek; and then she patted Lady on the head.

"So I got a raise, and I've already run all the numbers. We can afford to get a house now. And we can buy more than we can afford right now, because I'll be getting another raise soon, and possibly another promotion."

"Another promotion? How could you know that?"

"HR—you know, human resources—is a two-person department. Me and the manager. And the manager is looking to be moving on before too long. So if I do a good job—and I always do—I'll be up for his job."

"Sounds good, Dean." Angela forced a smile she didn't feel.

"I've already checked out houses online, and I want to show you one of them. It's not too far. Let's go look at it."

Angela figured it wouldn't hurt to look at it, so she nodded her head. "All right. When do you want to go look?"

"Now! I want to go now! I'm excited about getting our own house!" He stepped forward and put his arms around her. "Our *own* house!"

"What about dinner?"

"We'll go out! Come on, let's go." Dean stepped past her and opened the front door. Lady rushed out. "I guess Lady is going with us."

Angela closed the door behind her and dawdled toward the passenger side of Dean's car, where Lady sat, smiling and wagging her stub of a tail. "Come on, Lady. You get to go too."

Dean started chattering away at once, and instead of going straight to the house he had picked out, he had to take her on a house-hunting tour all around Thoreau. Some of the houses looked okay, and some not so okay. But the pounding in her head wasn't the beginnings of a headache. It was her heart saying, "No! No! No!" Until she made up her mind about actually staying with Dean, she wasn't going to even entertain the idea of buying a house with him. But until she decided, she would go along with him and look at houses.

"None of 'em have caught your eye, huh, Ange? Wait till you see the one I picked out. I'm telling you, it's perfect for us! Perfect, I tell you!" Then he laughed.

On the other side of town, he suddenly pulled over and turned off the engine. Angela looked at the house where he had parked. "It doesn't have a for sale sign, though, Dean."

He pointed at the big, blue house across the street.

"See?" he said. "It's even blue! Your favorite color!"

CHAPTER FORTY-SIX

DR. Weiss had another long, hard, enjoyable day at the clinic. He sat down in front of his computer and waited for his mail to appear on the screen. When it did, he smiled. Another email from Carla. But this was a surprise. *Daddy, Mom found a job! She's in a great mood, finally! And she's cooking dinner! Hope you can get home early to enjoy her good mood and dinner! Love you, C.*

Looking up at the doggie-doctor clock, he thought he'd have just enough time. He hurried out the door, started the car, and pulled away from the parking lot. Twenty minutes later he was home and pushing his way into the back door with his hands full. Wolf pushed up against him. "Sorry, Wolfie. I have my hands full right now." When he looked up, Helen was standing right in front of him. Her smile was so bright it almost knocked him off his feet. She stood with her hands on her hips.

"Well. Look who the cat dragged in. And he isn't even late. Will miracles ever cease?" She turned back to stirring something on the stove.

"Congratulations, Helen. Here." He put the box of candy on the already-set kitchen table and then searched for a vase for the dozen red roses he had bought her. She didn't like his flowers from the garden, but he thought she might like red roses bought from a florist. Helen didn't comment on either one. No "thank you." No nothing.

After putting the flowers in water and putting them as a centerpiece on the table, he walked up behind Helen, put his hands on her hips and kissed her on the cheek. She whipped around with a sneer on her face.

"Get away from me! I got a job! I don't need you anymore! I cooked you this dinner—your favorite—as a good luck gift. Good luck with your dinners from this point forward, because this is the last meal I'll ever prepare for you! Now sit down so I don't have to look at you anymore, or I may just leave everything to burn!"

He stepped back, shocked, but before he could even think of anything to say, Carla came into the room. "Oh, Daddy! What beautiful flowers you brought Mom. Aren't they beautiful, Mom?"

"I hate flowers!" Helen didn't even turn around.

"But I thought you loved roses?" Carla looked confused.

"I hate any flowers that your father brings me!" She pulled off her apron and stuffed it into Carla's hands. "Here. Everything is ready. You can serve the *pig*. I don't want to have anything to do with him ever again." Then she stormed from the room.

Carla looked at him with a surprised look on her face. "Gosh, Daddy. What did you say to her?"

He shook his head in disgust. "All I said was 'Congratulations, Helen' and then I put my hands on her hips and kissed her cheek." Shaking his head again, he continued, "That's when she exploded." Dr. Weiss shrugged. "Then you came in and—well, you know what happened after that."

This time, Carla shook her head. Then she put on the apron, grabbed two hot mitts from the wall, and served him his dinner. It wasn't until he sat down at the table that he realized there were only two places set. He might have seen it and thought it was for him and Helen. Now he wondered.

"Curt isn't home tonight. She meant this dinner for just me and you, Daddy, in case you're wondering." As sad as the situation was, Carla's reading his thoughts made him chuckle.

"You know me, don't you, sweetheart?" Dr. Weiss asked. Carla leaned over and kissed him on the forehead. Then he added, "And thank you for serving dinner. I could have done it myself."

"It's okay, Daddy. I don't mind. Maybe I can come home early from now on and try to fix dinner for you at night."

He smiled at her but shook his head. Carla was his darling daughter, but he had tasted her cooking before. It was as close to fast food as you could get without the golden arches. "No, thank you, hon. I'll figure something out."

They ate in silence for a few minutes, roasted lamb, baked potato, fresh broccoli: it *was* his favorite. And on the counter was apple pie. Helen had outdone herself for his "final dinner."

Carla stood up and poked her head out the door, then she returned, put her hand on his, and whispered to him. "Daddy, I think you should leave Mom."

174

CHAPTER FORTY-SEVEN

ANGELA leaned forward to look past him at the house across the street. Dean had a big grin on his face. Cars sped by at forty miles an hour. There were flowers along the edges of the house, and it looked like they continued all along the side that she could see. There was a big hedge in the back that may or may not have enclosed the yard. It was two stories and looked like it had a lot of light. But there was no way she would ever buy a house like that.

"Dean?"

"Yes, honey?" He still had a huge grin on his face. "It's perfect, isn't it? I mean, yeah, we need to see the inside before deciding, but I knew you'd love it!"

"Dean, I would never live in a house like that. You should know that."

"What do you mean? I thought you would love it." His grin turned into a concerned frown.

"This street is so busy. The cars are racing by. What about Lady?"

"The information online said it has a fenced yard. See? You can see part of the fence from here." Dean pointed at the hedge.

"What if she gets out in the front? What if she runs into the street accidentally?"

"Lady never gets out in the front!"

"Dean. She did today. As soon as you opened the door and she knew we were leaving, she ran straight out the door."

Without replying, Dean started the car and drove off. After a meal of fast food where he let her order for herself, he drove home, plopped himself in front of the television, and didn't say another word all night. Angela thought it was a pleasant change.

What she really thought was that they had been together for years and Dean did not even know this simple thing about her. She *never* wanted to live on a busy street. And it wasn't just because of Lady, although that was a huge piece for her. Angela liked tree-lined streets with children playing, she liked open fields and room to run. A busy street? She would as soon live on a freeway which, in her view, wasn't that different.

For the following week, Dean had not brought up looking for houses again. Most nights, he came home from work, plopped himself in front of the television, and watched sports until he went to bed. She realized how different their lives were, and she wondered how they ever had anything in common to begin with. Then Dr. Weiss came to mind. For days she had been focusing all her thoughts on finding out if he was married or not. Because she had come to a decision. If he was single— and interested—she would leave Dean and have no second thoughts about it.

176

When the time came for Lady's one month check-up, as Angela drove to the clinic in Berlin, she went over and over in her head a dozen different scenarios and what she would say in each one to find out if the good doctor was married or not. She could hardly wait to find out.

In the crowded waiting room Angela continued going over conversations in her head that would lead her to find out about the doctor's marital status. Her future depended on it. She was so focused on the virtual conversations in her head that Dr. Weiss had to call her name twice before she stood up and walked to the examining room with Lady.

"Daydreaming, huh?" asked Dr. Weiss.

Angela laughed self-consciously. "Yeah, something like that."

"So how's our little Lady today?" He kneeled down and looked into Lady's eye. "It looks good. Perfect. You still need to put the drops in her eyes. But otherwise, she's got the all-clear now!"

"So I still need to do the drops? All right."

"Oh, you probably need more. I'll get you some."

He turned around, went to the cabinet, and came back with the bottle in his hand. Before handing it to her, he stepped past Lady and close in front of Angela. She was so stunned by him walking right into her personal space that all she could do was hold out her hand and look up at him.

"Uh, thank you."

She thought she heard him chuckle before he took a step back. "So she's good to go now, and I don't need to see her again until she needs her shots."

"No shots for this girl, Dr. Weiss. But I will come in for titers."

177

"Ah, yes. More of that alternative medicine stuff."

"Exactly."

He stepped to the door, with a big smile on his face. "Okay, then, I'll see you next time then. Bye." And he disappeared out the door. It was then that Angela realized she never got the chance to find out if he was married.

CHAPTER FORTY-EIGHT

At the end of the day, after glancing at his empty email inbox, Dr. Weiss relaxed back in his easy chair thinking about his conversation with Carla. She hadn't mentioned it since then, and neither had he, but he had thought about her words a million times.

After hearing her say she thought he should leave Helen, he had said, "I thought when you were in the hospital and said that you didn't know why I let her talk to me like that, it was because of the drugs."

She had shaken her head. "No, Daddy, I'd been wondering for a long time why you put up with that. The drugs just gave me the courage to say it."

He stopped eating and looked down at his food. "And all this time, I thought you wanted me to stay with her. I thought you'd be furious with me if I left."

Carla put her hand on his and patted it. "Daddy, you need to leave her. You really do. It's not right to let someone talk to you like that—treat you like that. Curt and I have talked about it. We'd both be happier if you left.

179

The tension around here is awful!"

Even now, sitting in the easy chair and going over the conversation again in his mind, he still couldn't believe it had really happened. He had been allowing Helen to treat him like that, talk to him like that, for years, thinking he was doing it "for the children."

And come to find out that not only Carla, but Curtis, too, thought he should leave. The whole thing now made him feel guilty. He didn't worry so much about Carla— she was tough—but he wondered if he had just taught Curtis to stay in an unhappy relationship. What a horrible lesson to teach your son. Because Dr. Weiss wouldn't want anyone to go through what he had gone through these last few years.

Still, even after Carla told him he should leave and that she and Curtis would be happier if he left, he still wasn't sure it would be the right thing to divorce Helen. He had promised "till death do us part" when they got married, and he had always considered himself a man of his word. What kind of man would he be if he broke that promise?

He'd be a divorced man; and he never thought he'd be that. And he'd be alone. Dr. Weiss didn't like that idea at all. Even if the kids chose to live with him, they'd be starting college in a couple more years. Did he want to be all alone like that? Was it worth the abuse he was enduring just so he wouldn't have to be alone? That was something he'd have to give some serious thought. Although just being free from the abuse would be worth a lot to him. Maybe Helen'd be so busy working now that she wouldn't have time to scream and demean him anymore. There was always that.

Thinking of himself alone made him think of Angie.

Dr. Weiss still got a shiver when he even thought of her name. He tried to shake it off and not give it that much credence. It was ridiculous. Anything he didn't understand, he ignored.

But today—he had to laugh at himself—today he did something that was unexpected. While she was in the examining room with her dog, he had stood so close to her he could smell her hair. She must have just shampooed it, because it smelled of vanilla. He liked vanilla. And he liked her. He had put himself in her space, and he had to laugh at the way she reacted. She didn't move —he'd have to give her credit for that—but it shocked her to find him suddenly standing so close. So did that mean she didn't mind him in her personal space? Did that mean she *liked* him?

Dr. Weiss slapped the arm of his easy chair and chided himself for being so adolescent about the whole thing. "Does she like me?" he asked aloud in a falsetto voice. Did it even matter if she liked him? She was married, and he was not the kind of man to have an affair with a married woman—even if he was single. Oh, well. What made him hopeful was if he liked Angie—again that shiver that he couldn't control—maybe he could like someone else. Someone who wasn't already married. Someone single like he was soon to be. But *could* he really like someone else when he already had these feelings for Angie?

"Does *who* like you?" asked a voice from the other room.

CHAPTER FORTY-NINE

Sigrid started chattering away before the train ever moved. But Angelika found that the woman had such a pleasant demeanor that she didn't mind the company at all. When the train pulled away from the station and gained speed, Sigrid looked all around inside the car, and Angelika felt her shiver.

"I know this is Switzerland, and I'm safe here, but every time a train leaves the station like this, it always gives me the shivers." Sigrid rubbed her own arms up and down.

"Why?" Angelika wondered.

Sigrid looked around again and whispered, "Because I'm Jewish. And that's not a popular thing to be during these times. Switzerland is neutral now, but who knows how long that will last or how soon Germany will invade us?"

The woman's candor surprised Angelika. But they *were* in Switzerland. "Yes, I've heard the Germans are doing bad things to Jews." She had kept her own identity secret for so long that she said it without irony.

"Yes, I can confirm that it's true. I'm from there."

They had been speaking to each other in French, but when Angelika heard this, she switched to German. "Really? I am, too! I'm going home now."

Sigrid moved away from Angelika, and then with a big smile on her face, leaned forward and hugged her. "Hello, countryman! It's so good to speak my own language again!"

Angelika laughed. "Yes, I haven't even been away for a full day, and I miss it, too!"

Sigrid shrugged. "I wish I could have stayed, but I barely made it out as it was." She shook her head. "My parents and younger sister were all taken to Auschwitz. I don't expect to see them ever again."

"I'm sorry." Angelika patted the other woman's hand.

"I've come to terms with it. There was nothing I could have done. I got lucky. That's all it was. I wasn't home when the Germans came. And the German officer who raided my house was my boyfriend." She looked sharply at Angelika. "Wait. Before you think the worst about him, he had no choice. There was no warning at all. Somebody reported us. If I had been in the house with my family, I don't think he could have done anything for me either."

She stopped for minute like she was rethinking the whole episode. "But I was next door—at *his* parent's house, helping with his grandmother. When they heard the ruckus next door, they immediately hid me in a secret compartment in their house. Georg—now my husband —sent half his soldiers to the house on the other side of ours, and he and the rest of the soldiers came to his parents' house.

"It was a brilliant move, because if he hadn't done that, not only would he have been brought up on charges, but other soldiers would have come to search later, when we weren't prepared. Thankfully, the secret compartment kept me concealed, so the soldiers found nothing. Georg couldn't wait to get home that night to make sure I was safe." Sigrid shook her head again. "Enough about those sad times in my life. Tell me about you."

Angelika told her about her attorney-husband, Dieter, about attending college to become a psychologist, and about her ill-fated trip to Paris. She left out the confusion that drove her to make the trip by herself.

The two women continued their animated conversation until the train pulled into Bern two hours later. "Oh, I hate to say goodbye to you, Angelika! I feel like we've known each other forever!" Sigrid reached across the aisle and retrieved her bag. "Hey! Let me check the schedule! I have one right here—" She reached into her bag and pulled out a folded piece of paper. "Yeah! The train doesn't leave here for two hours! Come to my friends' house with me! You'll love them."

Angelika shook her head. "No, I'm not taking any chances, so I'm not straying far from the train. Sorry. I'd love to meet your friends, but after all I've been through, I need to get home."

"All right. How 'bout this? There's an all-night cafe right across the street from the train station. You can go there with me! I don't have to get to my friends' house right away. Come on! It will be fun! Better than sitting here in the station for two hours all alone! Come on!"

Angelika reluctantly agreed and followed the woman off the train, through the station, and across the street to an open-air cafe. It reminded her of the place where she had been headed when the bombs started falling in Paris. They sat under the single lighted table outside, and a sleepy-eyed, yawning waiter came out to ask what they wanted. It was dark outside and chilly, so Angelika ordered hot chocolate, and so did Sigrid. When the waiter brought the drinks, Sigrid waited for him to retreat into the building before leaning forward and whispering to Angelika.

"So I didn't tell you how I got out. Georg knew that not only I, but his parents had to leave so they wouldn't get in trouble for protecting me. Luckily, he had some good buddies that he could trust, and between them, they got me, his folks, *and Georg* out of Germany. It was done in such a way that no one got in trouble for it, although if Georg ever got caught, they'd throw him in Auschwitz."

"But he's here now, right? Safe in Switzerland? So they can't catch him, right?"

Sigrid looked down and scrunched up her napkin before looking up with tears in the corners of her eyes. "He's here—some of the time. That's why we live in Geneva—so close to the French border. So Georg can work with the Resistance in France. He risks his life every day trying to stop the Nazis."

"Oh, wow. That is scary."

Sigrid sniffled and looked at Angelika. "Tell me more about you, so I can get my mind off Georg. He says I worry about him too much."

That's when Angelika decided to tell Sigrid the whole truth about herself. All of it. She reached out and touched Sigrid's hand. "I have to tell you something." Sigrid nodded. Angelika leaned over and in a barely

185

audible voice lower than a whisper, she said, "I'm Jewish, too."

Sigrid's eyes got huge. "And you still live there? Are you crazy?" Before Angelika answered, Sigrid asked, "Does your husband know?"

"Yes, yes, he knows but nobody else does." Then she told her the whole story about her unmarried parents leaving her on the Schluters' doorstep. Sigrid nodded and encouraged her to go on. "And there's more, Sigrid. And you're the only one I can tell."

"Go ahead." Sigrid took a sip of her hot chocolate while staring at Angelika.

"My husband has a half-brother who is a Nazi officer."

"Your husband won't tell him, will he?" asked Sigrid.

"No, it's much worse than that." Angelika looked down at her hands and then up again to Sigrid. "I think I have feelings for him. And I think he has feelings for me."

"But this Nazi officer doesn't know you're Jewish, right?"

"Yes, that's right."

"Angelika, I don't know. If you tell him and you were wrong about his feelings for you, then you're—well, you're pretty much dead. And even if he has feelings for you, some of those Nazis—well, hate is stronger than love to them—you know what I mean?"

Angelika nodded. "Yes, I know. I don't think Rolf is like that though."

"Wow, that is some story. And I think you're caught in the middle. What are you going to do?"

"I have no idea." She took a deep breath and exhaled slowly. "I have no idea."

They talked for another hour about inconsequential

things, and then it was time for Angelika to get back on the train to Zurich. As they walked back to the station, Sigrid whispered into Angelika's ear, "Don't decide about your man before you find out how he really feels about Jews. And be careful!" Then they hugged goodbye, and as the train left the station Angelika waved to Sigrid as tears fell down her face.

CHAPTER FIFTY

ANGELA was so angry at herself about not getting the marriage question out there that she hit the steering wheel—which made her worry that she broke it—and scared Lady into cowering against the door and looking at her with sad eyes. "Sorry, Lady! Sorry!" She put her hand out petting the big dog's head and back. "I'm sorry. I won't do it again." Lady relaxed against the back of the seat and came away from leaning on the door. "I can't believe I didn't do it!"

Calming down after petting Lady, Angela thought about what had happened in the examining room and how disconcerted it made her when Dr. Weiss stepped right into her space. He got so close, she mused. He could probably smell her breath! Cupping her hand in front of her face, she exhaled and sniffed. Phew, she thought. It smells okay. But why did he do that? And she was certain she heard him laugh as he stepped back as if he had done that deliberately to put her off guard.

Did it mean that he liked her? Did it mean that he was

188

single? Although she had decided to leave Dean if Dr. Weiss was single and interested, this wasn't enough evidence to leave. What if she left, and he was married? Then where would she be? Alone, that's where she'd be. Alone and lonely. Oh, no, she couldn't leave on just the slight evidence of him stepping into her space and then laughing about it.

And when would she have another chance to find out? It was months before Lady needed her titers tested. Could she wait that long to decide about leaving Dean? She had to. There was no way she would wish something bad happening to Lady just so she could go see her doctor. That was a given. And Velvet the cat had no reason to visit a vet now, either. No, she'd just have to wait, which wasn't necessarily a bad thing. Maybe she and Dean could patch things up between them by then. Although she doubted that, at least it would give her more time to consider all the possibilities—all the scary possibilities.

It didn't take more than two weeks before Dean was not only chattering to her again but also complaining about his job. "I thought you liked it?"

"I'll like it a lot more when I'm the manager and there is someone under *me*."

"Is the manager abusing you in some way?"

"He treats me like I don't know anything! Like I'm a child!"

"But you just started in that department. He expects you not to know anything."

"You don't understand!" Dean flipped the television on and ended the conversation.

Before exiting the room and going into the bedroom to read, Angela stood there for a few minutes looking at

Dean. He couldn't see her, and the TV was too loud for him to have noticed that she didn't walk away. His outburst made her think about leaving him again. For some reason, it made it more real. It felt like their life together was fading away. Anything they might once have had in common felt like it was slipping away fast. So leaving felt more real to her and that scared her. Leaving Dean would mean a new life. She would have to leave almost everything she knew and everything she was, behind. If she found the courage to leave him, what would remain of her? That made her afraid. And the fear made her wonder if she could make it work with Dean. It made her wonder if leaving would be a huge mistake she would someday regret.

Then she remembered Dr. Weiss stepping into her space so easily. His eyes when he laughed. If she could feel this way about him, perhaps even if he was married, she could feel that way about someone else. But *could* she feel that way about someone else, she wondered. The connection with him felt so strong. Even mention of his dog—whom she had never met—sent shivers running down her spine. If he was married, then she could be in real trouble. Having left Dean behind and then being unable to fall for another man. *Then* what would she do? It suddenly became more imperative than ever to discover if the vet was married. Maybe she could just take Lady in to get her titers done a few months early.

CHAPTER FIFTY-ONE

DOCTOR Weiss, shocked when he realized someone else was in the clinic and had heard him, said, "Oh, I was just repeating something I heard on television last night."

Sheila, the night tech, had come in early. She laughed. "Yeah, right, Dr. Weiss. You're not a television watcher, I know that! You must have been talking about some cute poodle that came in today!"

He laughed. "No, Sheila, not a poodle. It was a Saint Bernard that was as cute as pie."

"Bye, Dr. Weiss. See you in the morning." She walked to the back of the clinic where she had a small room where she could sleep.

"See you tomorrow, Sheila."

Dr. Weiss drove to the Chinese takeout place for the third time that week. He needed to expand his horizons, he thought. But after he left the clinic, he felt too tired to experiment. Maybe he should become a vegetarian. That made him think about Angie again. Her husband had not come to the last few appointments. Maybe she and her husband had separated? If she was married, wouldn't she have moved when he stood so close to her invading her personal space? Or maybe he was just inventing reasons to keep her on his mind.

The more he thought about it, though, the more he decided that he didn't want to leave Helen. There'd be so many repercussions: the house, the children, Wolf. What if she fought to keep Wolf? What would he do then? He hadn't even thought about the dog before. The kids were old enough to fend for themselves, but what if she insisted on custody of the dog, and then didn't treat him well? Not that she had ever *mistreated* him, but Dr. Weiss was the one who made sure the dog was fed and watered—and loved. No, the more he thought about it, the more he realized that leaving would be the wrong thing to do.

And if he was staying—and he was—then he had to get the woman, Angie, off his mind. If that was even possible. He pulled into the driveway, gathered the boxes of Chinese food, and walked into the back door of the house. Wolf greeted him. No one was in the kitchen, but he could hear the television in the other room. The kids watched in their rooms if they watched at all. And Helen hadn't watched television in ages. So why would the TV be on? It didn't matter. All he wanted right now was to eat his dinner in peace with no insults or anger.

Wolf rubbed against his legs as he got a plate from the cupboard, so he leaned over and hugged the dog. "I'll never leave you, big guy. Never." He whispered in the big dog's ear, and the dog licked him across the face. "I love you, Wolfie, but I don't appreciate your wet kisses!" Dr. Weiss stood up and wiped off his face with a kitchen towel. That always angered Helen when she saw it, but, at this point, who cared?

He realized there was a certain amount of freedom that came with the end of a relationship—if that's what this was. Until one of them left, or said they were leaving, then he supposed he couldn't call it the end of a relationship, but it felt that way. Shoveling more of the Chinese food into his mouth, he just wanted to finish eating and get out of the kitchen. With the television on like that, he thought he was in imminent danger of being abused—again. And now that Helen had gotten a job and said she would never cook for him again, he didn't have to take that anymore. Nor did he intend to.

Putting the remainder of the takeout into the refrigerator, he rinsed his dish and silverware and stuck them in the dishwasher. Then he petted the big dog and asked if he wanted to go to sleep with him. Wolf wagged his tail and followed him out of the kitchen. He walked softly past the den and noticed that Helen was watching television with her head lolled over to one side like she was sleeping. Poor thing, he thought. She probably had a difficult day at work. It was funny, he realized when he acknowledged those thoughts, he still felt a certain amount of love and compassion for her. And yet, she seemed to have none for him.

Wolf followed him into the guest room where he had been staying since Helen announced that she would never cook for him again. He closed the door, and the dog jumped up on the bed where they had been sleeping together for several nights.

CHAPTER FIFTY-TWO

DAYS passed, weeks passed, and Angela forgot all about taking Lady in for titers early. And although she was very unhappy with her marriage to Dean, the thoughts of leaving him had weakened considerably. Or perhaps she should say *she* had weakened considerably. One day she and Dean had gone to a festival in town. When she looked around at the other men, she didn't think there was much out there to interest her. That's when she decided she should just stay where she was. Unhappy but attached. She just needed to stay married and shut up about any differences or difficulties between them. The thought of that almost made her feel sick to her stomach, because she didn't want to be there anymore.

And Dean had gone to *again* complaining daily about his job. Sometimes she thought she should have compassion for Dean because his job gave him a lot of grief. Although the bright spot was that he thought he would be promoted to personnel manager soon. But then, all of his jobs somehow escalated into giving him a lot of grief. She thought that he created that in his jobs all by himself. So how could you have compassion for that? Right now, she could barely manage compassion for herself for *having* to put up with a miserable, unfulfilling relationship.

Having to. Right. She could leave whenever she wanted, and she knew it. What was stopping her then? Her marriage was over. That much was clear. It was all over except for the shouting, as they say. And yet, she didn't have the courage to leave. If only she could catch him being unfaithful or something. But Dean wasn't that kind of man. And if she waited for that, she'd be with him forever. No, this was something she had to do on her own. It was like she needed more incentive. And the more she thought about it, the more she realized that the incentive she needed was knowing that Dr. Weiss was single.

Angela knew she would leave in a minute for Dr. Weiss, but she also knew that if he was married or not interested, then she probably wouldn't leave Dean. She'd just put up with her meaningless marriage until it was so horrible there was nothing left for her to do but leave.

There was something else that she had thought about. Sometimes she had the feeling it might be more difficult to leave Dean than she had expected it to be—that maybe he had more *power* over her than she had anticipated. She knew there was a time when she thought Dean was the love of her life. But she also remembered clearly that that thought didn't last too long. It had been abundantly clear for a long time now that he wasn't even close to the love of her life. Was there such a thing? That had been something she struggled with now and again.

Could that be Dr. Weiss? Angela shook her head. Not if he was married, it couldn't.

One Saturday morning, she had to work for a couple of hours. She had just finished a last email to her supervisor when her phone rang. It was Dean, and it was the call that changed everything.

"Ange, can you come home quick? Lady hurt herself. You need to take her to the vet."

"What happened? Dean! What happened? Tell me!"

"We were out playing and she ran over a rock. When she brought the ball back, I noticed that she was limping. She ripped off her whole toenail, and she's bleeding all over. Come quick! There's blood everywhere and I can't get it stopped."

"Can you make the appointment? Dr. Weiss in Berlin. Look it up. I'll be there soon!"

She locked up her office, ran out the door, and drove too fast all the way home. As she drove, she knew that although Lady's paw was bleeding, it wasn't that serious. She'd had dogs with broken toenails before, and it wasn't an emergency if you could get the bleeding stopped. But now she had the opportunity to see Dr. Weiss again. If he worked on Saturday, which she wasn't even sure about. Oh, no! What if Dean wanted to go with her? The way he carried on about Lady bleeding, he'd probably want to go. Oh, don't let him want to go, please don't let him want to go, she thought. When she got home, Lady, holding one paw up, was already on a leash, and Dean was standing on the porch, looking dejected, with blood all over his pants and shirt.

CHAPTER FIFTY-THREE

FOR a Saturday, it had been a slow day. That was all right with Dr. Weiss. Between fetching his dinner every night and sharing a bed with Wolf—the big dog took more than his share of room—he could use an easy day. Helen was still working and blissfully ignoring him, so that part was good. But figuring out his dinner every night had become a chore. He had even bought dinner a time or two at the health food restaurant in town. That gave him a chuckle.

Wouldn't Angie think that was funny? Him coming to her side. He wasn't convinced that so-called health food all fit into the "paleo" diet she advocated, but he was sure it was close. Dr. Weiss looked at the calendar on his desk and wondered how much more time had to pass before her dog Lady would need to get her shots. Oh, pardon me, he thought to himself. Her *titers* tested. That made him chuckle again.

Thinking about Angie made him think of his own marriage—if you could call it that. It hadn't been a real

197

marriage in years, and now it was only worse. And even after he had gotten "permission" from Carla to leave the relationship, he still couldn't do it. He thought that would make him a failure, and Dr. Weiss did not like being a failure. But leaving or not, the marriage was over, so did it matter? Wasn't he *already* a failure? Or were he and Helen *both* failures? Because a marriage included both partners, didn't it? And if that marriage failed, then it was both partners' faults, right?

Unless there was infidelity or addiction or something, then that might make a difference. But he imagined there were exceptions to everything. Carla never said it was his fault. She just thought he should leave, and after Helen's outburst the other night, he was certain that Carla didn't want him to leave to *protect* her mother. *He* was the one who needed protecting. Regardless of whose fault—

"Dr. Weiss?" A voice from the door interrupted his thoughts.

He looked up from his reverie. "Yes, Megan?"

"I didn't know if you had checked your schedule again. Someone called and made an appointment for eleven."

"All right, thank you. Who was it, do you know?"

"I can look if you want. All I know is it's someone with a Rottweiler."

"That's fine. It doesn't matter. Thanks for letting me know."

Megan walked away and left Dr. Weiss wondering. Because he had several clients with Rottweilers, he had no reason to think this client was Angie, but he hoped that it was. Looking at the doggie-doctor clock, he smiled at the time. Ten-thirty. He wouldn't look it up on the computer. He would wait and see. It was only half an hour. He smiled again. It was almost as if he could feel her hurtling through time and space toward him. How ridiculous he thought. Now he was getting carried away.

At ten fifty-five, he heard a dog enter the room next to his office, and he knew it was the Rottweiler. Whether it was Angie or not, he would find out in a minute. But he had a feeling that it was—a strong feeling. So when he walked into the examining room and saw her, it did not surprise him.

"Good morning, Angie, Lady!" Dr. Weiss couldn't help the big grin on his face.

"Good morning, Dr. Weiss," Angie said with a hesitant smile.

"What's going on with Lady today?" He looked down at the dog and saw her holding up one paw. "Oh, it's your paw, Lady? Let me take a look." Dr. Weiss kneeled down and cradled the paw in his hands. "Ouch! That looks like it hurts. Hold on a minute, I'll be right back." He dashed out the doorway and came back a minute later with a warm rag.

"We'll fix you up in no time, Lady." He cleaned carefully around the broken nail and examined it more closely. "Did it bleed a lot?"

"Yes, but—your receptionist said to put instant coffee crystals on it, and that worked."

"Okay, that's good. Corn starch or styptic powder will work, too, but I don't think this will bleed anymore. Although that all depends on Lady." Dr. Weiss stood up and rummaged through the cabinet behind him and brought back antibiotic ointment. "Here, Lady, this will help, too." He rubbed it on the broken nail. When he stood up, he handed the ointment to Angie. "Put this on three times a day. Do you think she needs an E-collar?"

"Is that one of those lampshade things?" asked Angie.

Dr. Weiss chuckled. "Yes. One of those."

"No, I think she'll be fine without it."

"All right, just one more thing then. I'd like to give her oral antibiotics to cover all our bases." He turned around to get it until Angie called him back.

"Dr. Weiss? This is antibiotic cream, isn't it?"

"Yes, but I prefer to be extra careful with a nail injury."

"I'd rather not add to the antibiotic resistance in the world, so I'll decline those." When he looked at her skeptically, she added, "I'll watch the nail carefully, and if I see any indication at all of infection, I'll call to get a prescription. I promise."

"Or you could come in to pick it up." He hoped that didn't sound too forward.

She nodded and then looked at him funny with her head tilted. "Can I ask you something?"

"Sure, ask away." He thought it would be about antibiotics or something.

"Who cooks for you?"

The question made him take a step back. "What?"

"I asked, who cooks for you? I thought you ate out all the time, but you described a healthy dinner. And you said you don't cook. So who cooks for you?"

He turned away from her and said, "I eat out all the time."

"No, come on. Who cooks for you?"

"I eat out a lot."

"Dr. Weiss, who cooks for you?" It was almost demanding. She felt bad, but she had to know.

Dr. Weiss looked down and couldn't meet her eyes.

"My wife." When he said it, he thought he saw her stagger back. Angie stayed quiet, and only because he couldn't think of anything else to say, he said, "Why hasn't your husband come in with you lately?"

It looked as though she was blinking back tears. "Because I left him."

Surprised, Dr. Weiss took another step backward, and his eyes opened wide. "Oh! When was that?"

"As soon as I get home."

CHAPTER FIFTY-FOUR

Sigrid had already left the station when Angelika discovered there was an issue with the train, and it was leaving an hour later than scheduled. Although she didn't even know what time the train from Zurich to Munich left, she was grateful that she would be on it or the next one and be home soon. Friends from college had family in Zurich, so she knew trains left from there regularly. When the train finally left the station, she had started feeling sleepy again. It pulled into Zurich at nine o'clock, and she exited the train hoping that the next train for Munich would be soon.

When she arrived at the ticket window and said she wanted to buy a ticket for Munich, the clerk shook his head. He explained there was an issue with the tracks between Zurich and Munich, and she could only get there through Salzburg, Austria. Angelika felt devastated. The trip from Zurich to Munich was only a four hour train ride. But now it would take her six hours to get to Salzburg, and another two hours to Munich, with who knows how much of a wait between trains. The train to Salzburg didn't even leave for three more hours, so that was another delay. Angelika shook her head in despair—blinking fast to keep from crying—and bought the ticket to Salzburg.

She had to wait in the station nearly three hours before boarding the train to Salzburg. Angelika thought of venturing out into Zurich, but didn't want to take any chances on missing the train. She'd been gone too long already and craved the safety of her own home. And to see Rolf. Somehow she needed to find a way to tell him she was Jewish. Although she knew she was taking a big chance in telling that to a Nazi, she still knew she needed to do it. If it wasn't meant to be with him, and she wasn't certain of that, then perhaps she'd end up in one of the Concentration Camps. Perhaps she'd end up dead.

And she didn't care. How strange it felt to think that thought. How many short months had it been since a Nazi officer had appeared at their door and frightened her? And now she was so in love with him she didn't want to live without him—? She was willing to risk everything she had, everything she was, *for him*. For his love. Angelika shook her head, because she didn't understand those feelings at all. And yet that wasn't to say that she didn't feel them down to her soul. There was not one doubt in her mind she had to face Rolf and confess to him she was Jewish.

Wait. Confess like it was a bad thing to be Jewish? No, she would *tell* Rolf, with no apology at all. It *wasn't* a bad thing, even though everyone all around her thought so. All of Germany hated Jews because of Hitler and his SS men. She laughed at the joke that wasn't funny—she was in love with one of the SS men.

203

How could this happen to an intelligent, thinking, discerning woman such as herself? It was crazy. She had no business being in love with anyone but her husband, and yet this had happened.

What would Freud say? He'd probably say it was sexual. What would Jung say? He would probably say it was meant to be. And that's what she thought. If something so peculiar could happen to her, then it must have been meant to be. What other explanation was there for her feelings? And it wasn't just feelings. It was *beyond* feelings; it was a *connection* she felt to Rolf. Perhaps it was because the dog had brought them together. But she knew she felt a strong connection with Rolf that she had never felt for Dieter.

By the time the train boarded for Salzburg, Angelika had thought of a hundred ways to tell Rolf, and a hundred reasons each one wouldn't work. And on the train chugging her way to another intermediate destination, she pulled out Jung's book again. When she held it in her hands, it opened by itself to the chapter on synchronicity —which meant nothing to her—until she read Jung's definition again. *Events are "meaningful coincidences" if they occur with no causal relationship, yet seem to be meaningfully related.*

Shrugging her shoulders, she was about to turn to another chapter, when it hit her. Meeting Sigrid! Was meeting Sigrid a synchronicity? Sigrid was a young Jewish woman in love with—and now married to—a Nazi. And Angelika herself was a young, Jewish woman in love with a Nazi. Was it a meaningful coincidence? Yes, very meaningful. But it wasn't an event, and so she didn't think that it applied. The only way it would apply was if there was another event related to meeting Sigrid.

She closed the book in disgust of her grasping at anything to make a horrible situation tolerable.

CHAPTER FIFTY-FIVE

ANGELA backed out of the examining room after bumping into the door, but she didn't look at him again. She paid the receptionist and hurried out the door. Barely maintaining her composure, she put Lady in the car and followed her in. Then she put the key in the car without starting it, rested her head against the steering wheel, and burst into long, wracking sobs. Lady kept licking her ear to make her feel better.

She didn't know how long she sat there, sobbing, but after a while the tears let up. Then she did some deep breathing and tried to get herself together. What happened in there was unexpected—not the part about his wife—but the part about leaving Dean. All this time she had thought and thought and decided that unless Dr. Weiss was single and interested, she would just stay with Dean.

But when Dr. Weiss had said "my wife," everything inside of her—everything she had been pushing down for months or even longer—had come unhinged. What

206

she said about "as soon as I get home" had popped unbidden out of her mouth. And now, thinking about it, she knew—knew down to the marrow of her bones— that was the right thing to do. In that moment when everything she had held onto for all this time had disappeared, she knew it was what she *must* do. In the clarity of her post-sobbing self, she recognized that when he said "my wife," in that moment she knew that although she had nothing left to run to, she still wanted to run. And if she wanted to run *that* bad, then that's what she must do.

Then she remembered what happened after she arrived at the house to get Lady. She had walked up to Dean and Lady on the porch, and he handed her the leash. Despite her not even wanting him to go to the veterinary clinic with her, she couldn't help but ask him if he was going.

"You're going with, right?" She had asked while bending down to examine Lady's sore paw.

"No. She'll be fine with you. And I need to change clothes, anyway. I can't be seen out like this." Dean pointed toward his bloody clothes.

"I can wait. It won't take you long to change."

Dean turned toward the door and opened it. "No, you can handle it. Right?"

"You have a game to watch, don't you?" She walked Lady toward the car. Without even answering, Dean had entered the house and let the door slam behind him.

Shaking off the memory that irked her, she started the car, pulled out of the parking lot, turned left at the light, and drove down the highway toward home—or what had been her home since she and Dean had moved to Thoreau. Who would leave once she told Dean their relationship was over? If he wanted to stay at the house, she would have to find a place that allowed dogs, for surely Dean would not want to keep Lady.

He'd grown to love Lady, sure, but Angela didn't think he'd loved her that much. And she didn't think he was the kind of man who would want to keep Lady for spite just because he'd know Angela wanted her. Or *was* he that kind of man? She suddenly remembered all kinds of horror stories of friends whose husbands did all kinds of irrational things unlike them after the women left them. Would Dean react like that? Was she in danger of losing Lady to Dean's anger or vengeance? She'd fight for her, she knew that. If Dean did try to get Lady, she could say she wanted Velvet, who had been his before they met. She hoped it wouldn't come to that though. But right now the most important thing was to get as far away from Dean as she could.

Angela still couldn't get over Dr. Weiss trying to get out of telling her he was married. Why would a man try to do something like that? Maybe he wasn't the man she thought he was. It was too bad. They did have some kind of connection—she still didn't understand what it was— but she knew it was there, because she could *feel* it. Still. Even knowing he was married, she could still feel the connection between them.

And she also knew that she had matured enough in herself to realize that if she was in a relationship with Dr. Weiss, even if he had to stay late at the clinic, it would be okay. Because she would know that when he got home, they would have more quality time together than she had ever had with Dean. Their time together was just time, not quality time.

As she drove down the highway approaching home,

tears streamed down her cheeks again. None of it mattered anymore. Dr. Weiss was married! How could she possibly have had those intense feelings for a man who was married? What was the design behind that? How could something like that even happen to her? She didn't understand, and she wasn't sure if she even wanted to understand it.

Was Dr. Weiss supposed to be a catalyst in her life—her feelings for him convincing her that she needed to leave Dean? No! It wasn't an infatuation; she felt certain of that. It was so much more. By the time she parked in front of their house, she had barely managed to stop the tears.

Dean must have heard her car pull up, because he came out the door. "Is she going to be okay?"

"Yes, Dean, she'll be fine. Come inside, we need to talk."

She walked into the living room, used the remote to turn off the television set, and sat on the couch. He sat on a chair opposite her.

"What's wrong?" he asked. "You said Lady's okay, right?"

"Lady will be fine, Dean. But we won't. We aren't okay, and we haven't been okay for a long time. I want a divorce."

"Because of what happened to Lady today? It could have happened to anybody! I didn't want to hurt Lady! You know that!"

Angela placed her hand on top of Dean's to comfort him, but he pulled it away. "Dean. It has nothing to do with Lady. It has to do with you and me and how we don't fit together anymore. I'm sorry. I'm done." She stood up and went into the bedroom to read, leaving

Dean in the living room with silent tears welling in the corners of his eyes.

CHAPTER FIFTY-SIX

Dr. Weiss stood in the examining room after Angie and Lady left the room. He was floored. He had experienced nothing like this in his life. What had Angie done to him? So she left her husband. No! She was *going* to leave her husband when she got home today. What was that about? What in their conversation had convinced her to take an action like that? And the reason he asked himself that was because he had a feeling that was not her intention when she walked in there. But there was no time to think about it now—he had heard someone enter the examining room next door. His patients were waiting. As he walked out the door, he caught Megan as she hurried by him.

"Megan, please tell Kelsey no more appointments after one o'clock unless it's an absolute emergency."

"Got it, Dr. Weiss." She moved around the corner.

The following two hours were a blur to him. One patient after another, and thankfully, he knew every one of them that came in, which made it easier. Nothing complex to speak of, and although Kelsey had already made an appointment at one-fifteen, that was the last one. Usually, he encouraged her to make appointments later than his one o'clock closing time just so he could stay longer and not have to go home. Today, though, he needed to think.

At one-thirty, he retired to his office and sat in his easy chair. His emails could wait. Kelsey left at one-forty-five, and Megan left at two o'clock, leaving him all alone in the clinic except the animals. Sheila wouldn't arrive until four. He had plenty of time to go over the conversation with Angie. Or so he thought.

Sheila showed up at four, and he hadn't even begun to process what had happened in the examining room. He caught her up with what the animals needed, and she withdrew to the back room. She was an introverted woman more at home with animals than people. Just like he was, but his job had forced him to become more outgoing, and he had adapted well.

Feeling self-conscious, he closed the door to his office although Sheila was way in the back, and he wasn't doing any talking anyway. But he felt more at ease thinking these uncomfortable thoughts when he was all alone.

It had started with her question about who cooks for him. He had tried to get out of answering it, but she wouldn't let him. And then when he had answered that it was his wife, he could have sworn that she had staggered back when he said the words.

And he felt so disconcerted with the exchange that he had said the only thing that popped into his mind: asking about her husband. Was that inappropriate? No, he didn't think it was, because he had the feeling she knew the answer to the question about who cooked for him before he ever uttered a response. But when she demanded an answer while he side-stepped the question, why did she stagger back if she already knew the answer?

It was all so confusing. And the most confusing of all was why he even answered that it was his wife who cooked for him. The truth was that Helen did not cook for him anymore and hadn't for weeks. So why did he feel obliged to answer like that? Because she expected that answer? Or because he felt embarrassed to say he did eat out every night now? Or because he was afraid of what might happen if she knew he ate out every night? That's why he had tried to make a joke of it until she pressed him.

What might happen? Although his marriage was over, and although Carla had told him he should leave, if he *didn't* leave, and he wasn't intending to—at least he wasn't intending to when he came to work that morning —there would be no way he would ever be unfaithful to his wife, nor would he make a woman unfaithful to her husband. It not only wasn't right, but there was no future in that. Future? Hmmm. His everyday life at the clinic was happy, peaceful, and fulfilling, but he had no future. For the last several years since their marriage had fallen apart, there had been no future.

Did he even need one? He wondered what it would be like to come home from work to someone whose eyes sparkled when she saw him, someone interested in his day, someone he could talk to who would listen. Angie was leaving her husband. Was *she* the one who could do those things?

That made him wonder. It had now been five hours since she had been at the clinic, and it would only take her an hour to get home. Had she told him yet? Had she changed her mind? Maybe his answer about his wife unsettled her, and she said that about leaving her husband when she didn't mean it. But why would she say it if she didn't really mean it? How could he find out if she meant it or not—told him or not?

Why would it matter? Dr. Weiss would not leave Helen no matter what. There was something in him that prevented that—even though he didn't know what it was. If Angie did divorce her husband, would that be enough incentive for him to leave? Dr. Weiss shook his head and would have screamed if he'd been at the clinic alone, although that would have scared the animals, so it was just as well. He didn't know what to do! He didn't even know what he wanted to do. So he took a deep breath, relaxed back in his chair, and tried to figure out where to eat dinner.

CHAPTER FIFTY-SEVEN

It wasn't until the train pulled into Salzburg at six o'clock in the evening, and she had checked the schedule for when the next train left for Munich, *and* was waiting for the next boarding call that she realized she had not once thought to call Dieter to tell him that she was all right. Why hadn't she called him? Why? Because her head was full of fantasies about Dieter's brother Rolf.

Angelika would have liked to feel guilty about that, but there was something in her that she couldn't control. Her overwhelming love—and connection—with Rolf over-powered any loyalty she had to Dieter. It was out of her control. She hadn't meant to fall for Rolf and had never anticipated ever loving another man besides Dieter. What she felt for Rolf, though, was so far beyond *just love* that she barely knew what to call it. It was something beyond the two of them, beyond time, beyond space.

Angelika decided that since she would be home in three hours, she wouldn't call Dieter this late. She'd see him so soon anyway. And that made her wonder if Rolf would be at the house yet. Although he usually came on Friday evenings, sometimes he wouldn't come until Saturday morning. What day was it, anyway? So much had been crammed into a day and a half.

She had left Munich yesterday morning, arrived in Paris, got bombed, *got bombed* she repeated in her head with emphasis, took the train to Switzerland, met Sigrid, took the train to Austria, and now only thirty-three hours later she was returning to Munich. She would get back to the house no later than nine-thirty. All that in so few hours, she thought. Shaking her head, she rested it on the back of her chair. When they announced boarding, she stood up and walked to the train.

The train was about to pull away from the station when a woman appeared in the doorway between train cars. The woman's hollow, haunted eyes betrayed her as a Jew even before the black-outlined yellow Star of David sewn onto her chest did. Inside the star, printed in faux Hebrew letters, it said *Jude*. What the woman was doing going *back* into Germany was a mystery. Angelika had heard rumors that Germany had already begun deporting Jews into Poland. Perhaps this young woman was returning—foolishly—to visit family.

When the woman appeared, other people in the train who sat alone in two-person seats, began frantically moving their bags to the seat beside them to discourage the woman from sitting beside them. Everyone believed Jews were inferior, and no one wanted that to rub off on them. Nor did they want to risk anyone calling them a Jew-lover which often meant deportation to the camps alongside the Jews.

When Angelika looked at the woman and the woman locked eyes with her, she told herself she didn't want the

216

woman sitting next to her for the second reason. But the real reason was a fear greater than that. Angelika feared someone would find her out for what she was—not a Jew-lover, but a Jew herself. She did not move her bag over to the seat next to her, but she buried her head in her book to discourage conversation in case the woman sat down beside her.

But the woman didn't. Although she hesitated in the aisle at Angelika's seat, when Angelika didn't look up, the woman passed her by. An hour later when she thought the coast was clear, Angelika snuck a glimpse behind her. The young woman had sat on a single seat—if you could call it that—right in front of the doorway. It wasn't really a seat; it had no back and it was taller than a seat. Sometimes people would use that spot to open their luggage and get something out. When Angelika looked back, the woman was staring right at her.

Angelika turned her head forward and tried to forget those empty eyes. But they weren't easy to forget. Those eyes could be *her* eyes if her life had gone differently. Depending on what would happen in the coming days, they could *still* be hers. That thought gave her a sick feeling in her stomach. If she was that unsure of Rolf, how could she be so in love with him? And yet she was.

The rest of the two-hour chugging train ride, she tried to convince herself to forget the whole thing. Forget Rolf, forget love, forget confessing—no, she meant to tell him she was Jewish. Forget everything, remain married to Dieter, and just go on living as she had been before she ever met Rolf. But could she ever be happy again knowing that Rolf existed in the world? She was fine while she had never met him, but now that she had met him and gotten to know him—and love him—she would never be the same again. And yet, and yet, she felt she needed to be strong and ignore her feelings. It was the only way she could *survive* the rest of her life—with Dieter, a man she loved, but whom she was not in love with.

That was her final decision when the train stopped and she stepped away from the platform hoping that she wouldn't see that Jewish woman again, ever again. Right now, there was no Rolf, there was only Dieter. Angelika would live with that. She would be semi-happy—happy enough—and comfortable and secure, and that would be enough. And *enough* would have to be enough for her.

As she walked home from the station, she felt a certain comfort in her decision. She didn't need Rolf to be happy, she would be fine without him. The more she repeated it to herself, the more she felt like she could believe it. And then she approached the house and saw Rolf's car parked in front. Although her courage and determination sagged, she held her head up high and walked through the front door.

There were voices in the kitchen yelling at each other —Dieter and Rolf. The only one who met her at the door was Wulfie. As she kneeled down to hug him, the voices from the kitchen became clear.

"You should have known they would bomb Paris! You could have warned her not to go!" It was Dieter's voice.

"I am a dog trainer, Dieter. The Führer does not consult me when he decides to bomb another country," Rolf answered without rancor.

"You're a Nazi! I'm sure you knew!"

"Dieter, if I knew, don't you think I would have told you? She is *your* wife after all."

Those words seemed to cement her resolve once more. So that's what he thought of her. Dieter's wife. After her harrowing ordeal in Paris and now hearing the comment that devastated her, Angelika was too upset to face the two arguing men. So she kissed Wulf on the top of the head and quietly took the stairs to the bedroom. Wulf lay down outside the door while she unpacked her clothes from her travel bag. She heard a door slam, and when she heard footfalls on the steps, she assumed it was Dieter coming to bed, but then she heard Rolf's voice.

"Wulfie? I was wondering where you'd gone." Then he must have seen the light from the bedroom. "What are doing up—" He stepped in front of the bedroom door and saw her standing there looking at him. "Angelika! You're alive!" Rolf held out his arms, and she fell into them, her resolve gone for good.

CHAPTER FIFTY-EIGHT

IT took Dean a week to move out. After finding his own apartment, which he did almost immediately, he still had to pack his things and move them, while working full time. Angela helped when she could, but she was working full time, too.

There had been no argument over who would keep the rental house, because Dean said he wanted to be closer to work. And he had also said he knew Lady was more Angela's dog than his, so he wouldn't try to get "custody" as he called it, with a brief smile. He had also asked if he could occasionally come over and take Lady out for the day and spend time with her, which Angela agreed to right away. She didn't think it would ever happen, but if he wanted to, that was fine. And he took their cat, Velvet, who had been his cat before they met.

Dean had only tried to talk her out of the breakup once. "Is there anyone else?" he had asked.

"No," she answered truthfully, but still felt like she was lying.

"And are you sure we can't work this out?" He had a sad, pleading look on his face.

"Dean, you already know we can't. This has been coming for a long time now—since before we ever moved here."

Dean looked down and shook his head. "Will you stay in New Hampshire?"

Angela shrugged her shoulders. "I don't know. I have no plans to leave right now. Will you stay?"

Dean shrugged, too, and then went back to packing his belongings; the discussion summarily dismissed.

Leave New Hampshire? It was something Angela had never considered. Return to where they used to live? Why would she do that? Her old job was gone, and she didn't miss it. And she enjoyed her job here. They appreciated her, and that meant a lot to her.

And then she kept trying to push down the thought that wouldn't be pushed down. What if Dr. Weiss left his wife? He must not be happy with her or he would not have said he got his peace from the clinic. To Angela, that had meant that he didn't get peace at home. What else could it mean? And that time when he stepped right into her personal space like he belonged there? Would he have done that if he was happily married? Maybe. Some men were like that. But he didn't seem like a womanizer to her. No, she felt like it *meant* something. But deluding herself like that would just make her feel lonely, so she tried to push him out of her thoughts. *Tried* being the operative word.

Weeks later, sitting alone in the house, she realized that she didn't miss Dean. And she didn't miss turning on the TV to the sports station either. Although Dean took the big TV—with her blessings—and she was stuck with the small one, it didn't matter to her, because she wasn't much of a TV watcher. Her nights alone were pleasantly silent and not filled with Dean's insistent chatter or the crowd roaring for a sports event he was watching. She was grateful for that.

Lady helped her not to feel so alone in the big house. Lady was a big girl and a big presence and got more than her share of hugs. It wasn't like Angela was missing hugs, because Dean had never been big on hugs anyway. Dean hadn't been good at many things that Angela felt she needed in her life: hugs, conversation, and holding hands to name a few. Sometimes she wondered why she had ever married him.

So it wasn't until her fifth weekend alone that it hit her. Dean was gone and he was gone for good. Was she sorry? No, but she did—for half a second—consider calling him and inviting him over. But she knew that would be the wrong thing to do. He would think it was an invitation to return home when all she needed was *temporary* company.

Ironically, she felt lonelier for Dr. Weiss than she did for Dean. And although she had never seen Dr. Weiss anywhere other than his clinic, she felt a deep longing for him. She missed him more than she missed Dean, although she didn't want to admit that.

It was silly because Dr. Weiss had never been in her life—her personal life anyway. That's not to say she hadn't spent many hours—and hours—thinking about him before her last visit. But once he had told her he was married, she had not allowed herself to think about him even once. That is, until Dean left, and then Dr. Weiss somehow intruded himself back into her thoughts. Angela knew it was wrong to think about him, not in the moral sense, but in the sense it was not doing her any good thinking about a married man. She needed to boot him out of her thoughts for good, and in a few more months she might consider dating.

CHAPTER FIFTY-NINE

WEEKS passed and summer turned to fall. Dr. Weiss couldn't remember how long it had been since Helen had found a job and stopped fixing him dinner. He had grown tired of pizza and Chinese food, and even the health food store had lost its appeal, so he bought a cookbook with simple ingredients and started cooking for himself. Both Carla and Curtis told him they had somewhere else to eat, but he had a feeling it was because of the one time he had tried cooking several years before when Helen went back East to see her family. That time he had added way too much pepper, not enough sea salt, and overcooked the chicken to the point that it was nearly inedible.

His cooking was much better now, although he had to admit that he had a few false starts in the beginning. He had burned a couple of dinners when he forgot to set the timer; another time he had set the timer but had forgotten to turn the oven on; and another time he had made a splendid spaghetti sauce, but had forgotten to cook the spaghetti noodles.

But all that was in the beginning. He had it down now. Usually he cooked on the weekends and made enough so he could freeze separate portions and then defrost them during the week. And his cooking wasn't bad at all—it may not have been as good as Helen's, but at least it was edible.

One time, he had gotten home and Helen was sitting at the table eating what he had left out for himself. As he walked into the room, she put the last bite in her mouth and stood up. "That wasn't half bad, Ralph. You're learning." She gave him a brief smile, rinsed the dish off, put it into the dishwasher, and walked out without another word.

Helen had been so cordial, that it made Dr. Weiss wonder if she would invite him back into sharing her room again, but she never did. He continued sleeping in the guest room with Wolf and continued cooking for himself.

When she saw him, she was always cordial, but she never had a conversation with him lasting more than one or two sentences. While she occasionally gave him a brief smile, she never talked to him about her job, nor would she answer if he asked her a question about it. She would just leave the room with the question unanswered. At some point, he stopped asking. Once he asked Carla and Curtis if she had said anything to them about the new job, but she ignored their questions, as well. But they both said it agreed with her, because she treated everyone much nicer.

None of it mattered though. Helen showed no indication of leaving, and there was no way he would leave first —even though Carla had given him her blessing to do so. He just couldn't do it.

There was something stopping him, something big. It was as if he felt like something dreadful—really dreadful —would happen if he left her. It felt so bad he didn't even like to think about it. Dr. Weiss had no idea what the dreadful thing could be. It was only this nebulous feeling more than anything else. And there was no way he would mess with that feeling. If he had to stay in a loveless marriage the rest of his life, then that was his fate, and he would accept that.

Dr. Weiss moved his head from side to side. He hoped that wasn't the case, but he knew of no way around it. So what he did in the meantime—though he realized that "meantime" could go on forever—was to think about the woman, Angie. After the last time he saw her when she had asked him about cooking and had told him she was about to leave her husband, he had looked up her telephone number more than a dozen times, tempted to call her and tell her the truth. What was the truth? Yes, Helen no longer cooked for him, but he was still married to her. And he was certain, after having spent several hundred hours analyzing the conversation, that was the question she was really asking.

Now it had been so long—was it months already?— that she had probably met someone else. But would the divorce be final as soon as that? Certainly she would wait until the divorce was final to start dating. Wouldn't she?

Perhaps she was like those women he had met before where the day after they separate from their husbands, they are already attached at the hip to someone else. Was Angie like that? He didn't think so. What he really thought, although he didn't like to dwell on it in case he was wrong, was that the two of them had a *special* connection, and that she would recognize that. Was that just a delusion? Wishful thinking? It didn't feel like a delusion, though, it felt real. But how long would Angie wait for him? It could be years before Helen made a move to leave. It could be never.

CHAPTER SIXTY

ANGELIKA stood by the front window gazing out into the pouring rain. She had one hand splayed over her heart and the other hand on the dog's head. And while she waited for Rolf to return, she went over the events of the last week.

When she came home from Paris that night, Rolf had hugged her tighter than anyone had ever hugged her and whispered "I love you, Angie."

Angelika had pulled away from him and looked into his eyes. "I love you, too, Rolf. But I need you to know something about me. I'm a Jew."

A smile creased his face, and he kissed her gently first on the lips and then on each of her eyes. "I don't care. I love you, Angie, like I've never loved another."

They stood there just gazing into each other's eyes, until Dieter walked up the stairs and saw them. "Angie! You're safe!" Dieter ran up to her and pulled her out of Rolf's arms and hugged her. "I can't believe you're alive and safe! Rolf! She's safe! She's safe!" He had guided her into their room and closed the door behind them, leaving Rolf in the hallway alone.

It wasn't until breakfast the following morning when Dieter was cooking eggs and chattering on about how happy he was that Angelika was safe that he turned around and saw them. Angelika and Rolf were sitting across the table from each other, their hands extended, but not touching, and gazing into each other's eyes, when it suddenly registered with Dieter what he had seen upstairs the night before.

At once he dropped the pan of eggs on the floor. When Angelika and Rolf turned around to see what had happened, Dieter stood there with his hands on his hips. "I see." He looked from one to the other. "I see what's going on, and it will stop now." He took two steps and put his hands on Angelika's shoulders. "She's my wife, Rolf, and you better leave right now. You go home to your wife, Helga, and your two sons, Karl and Kurt. Go on. Get out of my house. You're not welcome here anymore!"

Rolf's face clouded with confusion, but he stood up. Angelika saw him glance at her with a mix of apprehension and fear, but she had already burst into tears and then covered her face with her hands. She heard him click his heels together and walk from the room and up the stairs. Dieter called after him. "And don't come back here, Rolf. Ever!" Angelika ran from the kitchen, and since she could not run up the stairs into her room because Rolf had gone that way, she ran outside into the back garden and didn't return into the house until she heard Rolf's car drive away.

When the dog beside her shifted, interrupting her thoughts, she knelt down to hug him. "Don't worry,

Wulfie, he'll be back soon. He promised." Then she stood up and returned to what had happened.

For the following week after finding out that Rolf was married, she cried every day, and Dieter ignored her. On Friday, she had been staring out the back window watching the rain fall into the garden when she heard the front door open. Thinking it was Dieter, she remained where she was.

When the dog ran up and pushed himself against her leg, she resisted the urge to pet him. Instead she stood still and didn't move. Angelika heard Rolf's footsteps and then felt his hands resting on her shoulders, but she didn't react except to shrug his hands away. "Angie, I know I should have told you, but when did I have time? Honestly, when? And I'm sorry; I'm so, so sorry, but I said what I meant. I have never loved another like I love you. That is the truth."

She turned then to face him and crossed her arms across her chest. "But you're married! I have no interest in a married man!"

Rolf smiled then and touched her cheek. "Isn't that kind of a hard line for a woman who is already married —?"

That broke her. Tears erupted from her eyes and she reached up and put her arms around him. "What are we going to do, Rolf? What are we going to do?"

He pushed her away from him so he could look into her eyes. "I'll tell you what we will do. I am driving to my house now and telling Helga that I will not be returning. Ever. I will kiss the boys goodbye." At that moment, he choked up and had to look away. Rolf took a deep breath and then continued. "And then I will drive back here, and you and I will tell Dieter *together*. I think it will be easier on you that way. Yes?"

Angelika nodded. "Yes, Rolf. Thank you. That will be much easier for me." She wrapped her arms around him again. "Please don't stay away too long. I can't bear it."

"Don't worry. We'll never be apart again. I will arrange for us to leave Germany together so you never need to worry about your secret again." He kissed her on the top of her head. "I'll drive home tonight and tell Helga either tonight or tomorrow morning—I'd like to spend time with the boys before I say anything. And then I'll drive straight back here to you—and Beowulf—I'm leaving him here with you. I'll be gone less than twenty-four hours! Promise! By this time tomorrow, we'll be together! Forever!"

He had patted the dog, kissed her softly on the lips, and driven away into the rain. When Dieter had come home that night, he took one look at the dog, grunted, and walked away.

Now, almost twenty-four hours later, there was still no sign of Rolf's car in the rainy afternoon. How much longer would she have to wait? Had he changed his mind? Could *Helga* have threatened him with something so he couldn't return? Had his two young sons changed his mind? Angelika wasn't sure how much longer she could stand it. Kneeling down again to hug the dog to her, she heard the phone ring in the kitchen. She heard Dieter's muffled voice. A few minutes later, he walked into the room.

"You can keep the dog."

Angelika kept her face buried in the dog's fur and didn't look up at him. "What do you mean?"

"He's gone, Ange. Rolf is gone."

Now she looked up. "What do you mean he's gone?

You're just saying that."

"They found his car. In the bottom of a lake by a bridge. They think he braked suddenly to avoid a deer, lost control on the wet pavement, and slid into the lake. There was nothing they could do when they found him."

"I don't believe you." But she had an inkling he was telling the truth. Rolf should have been back to her by now.

"I'm sorry, Ange. You're welcome to go to the funeral with me tomorrow." Dieter turned and walked away.

And Angelika, crying into the dog's thick fur, knew her life would never be the same.

CHAPTER SIXTY-ONE

THE divorce felt so *final.* Angela didn't realize it would make her feel sad, but it did. They had filed a joint petition for uncontested no fault divorce. Two months later, they met in court and within a few minutes—since they didn't own a house and they agreed on everything else—the judge had declared their marriage dissolved. Before walking out of the courtroom, they had hugged, and just like that, their life together was finished forever.

In the time leading up to their divorce, Angela had moments of desiring Dean's *company*, but she had no second thoughts. And even her thoughts of his company faded fast when she remembered his constant talking and only occasional listening.

No, this was what she wanted—needed—regardless of her failure with Dr. Weiss. Well, it wasn't exactly a failure, it was more like a fantasy that stayed a fantasy. The only problem was it had never felt like a fantasy. It always felt like it was *already* real—like they were already a pair. What a mistake she had made with that assessment! What had felt so real to her before now only felt like a bad dream—bad in the sense that it was something she wanted that was always just out of reach, never attainable. How could she have deluded herself like that? It was as if she had bet her whole life on a connection she felt was real that turned out not to be real. So she lost the bet, and now she was alone and lonely.

But she hadn't really lost the bet, because for a long time she had needed to leave Dean. She had never had the courage to do it. Dr. Weiss—or the fantasy of a *connection* with Dr. Weiss—provided the catalyst she needed to change her life. And she knew without thinking about it that it was a change for the good of all. Dean was better off without her in his life. He just didn't know it yet.

What disturbed her was wondering if that was all that Dr. Weiss was. A catalyst? Was that it? Were those deep feelings she *thought* she had for him all bogus? A trick of her mind or something to assist her in doing what she was procrastinating about—leaving Dean?

After all these weeks that thought always made her feel sick to her stomach. Angela still had a deep longing for Dr. Weiss that she didn't understand. The longing felt deeper and more intense than anything she had ever felt for Dean. And no matter how many times she had tried to push Dr. Weiss out of her thoughts, he somehow always insinuated himself back in. It was as if it were out of her control. Sometimes she'd be busy doing something and suddenly a picture of him would pop into her head. What was that about?

None of it mattered though. He was married, and that was the end of that story. So when it came time for Lady to get her titers, she researched other vets in the area.

Although she felt confident that Dr. Weiss was a good vet, she didn't need to drive all that way to see a man who only made her feel bad about what she was missing. Feeling frustrated after finding something wrong with every vet she researched, she finally found one bordering on holistic. But when she called to schedule an appointment with her, the clinic told Angela that the vet had gotten married and moved to South Carolina!

Angela had to stop herself from throwing the phone across the room as if it were the phone's fault. She waited a week and then tried again. There were a few towns not far from Thoreau, so she researched those vets. The second one she saw on the internet *was* a holistic vet, and the website said all the right things. They even recommended titers over yearly shots. Perfect! She punched the number on her phone apprehensively, expecting to be shot down again. And she was. The holistic vet had retired six months earlier and had not taken the website down. He could not give her a recommendation for any other holistic vet around there.

It was as if the universe was conspiring against her. Why should she be forced to go see Dr. Weiss again when he was married? Why should life be so unfair? She was miserable enough trying to keep him out of her mind without having to see him and talk to him—without having him stand too close to her. But it was as if she had no other choice. All roads led to Dr. Weiss.

Angela fought it for two days trying to figure out what else she could do. And then one day it occurred to her— she had to go, and that's all there was to it. She knew if she delayed any longer she would change her mind, so she called that day for an appointment hoping to get in right away. And she was lucky—or maybe unlucky—

there had been a cancellation for his last appointment of the day. It wasn't a problem leaving work early to get there. She usually came in to work early and had comp time built up. So she'd see him that day. Great! No, bad! What was it, good or bad? That's how confused she was when she drove into his lot later that afternoon.

CHAPTER SIXTY-TWO

Dr. Weiss had a great day! It could not have started out any better. It felt like the first day of the rest of his life! Each one of his patients—and their owners—had been polite and entertaining. That's what he loved about his job, he could help animals and their owners and enjoy them, too. His favorite part of the job was the intricate surgeries he performed, but the "good" owners —the ones who weren't careless or neglectful of their pets—were also enjoyable.

There was one other thing today he wondered about. All day it was like he had felt the presence of Angie, but it was past the time she usually came in; so he discounted it by thinking it was because he was having such a great day.

The rest of the afternoon flew by, with every minute filled. He either had no cancellations that day or had the slots filled back in. Some days were like that. Most days were busy, but some days he had not one minute to spare. When you loved your work, it was all good.

By late afternoon, his enthusiasm for his great day had still not waned. How could it? And with one patient to go, he had already decided that he would go out and celebrate that night. He deserved a celebration and even if he had to celebrate alone, it would still be a celebration. Grabbing the file as he walked into the examining room, he didn't have time to read the name before he looked up and saw her. Angie and her Rottweiler, Lady.

With a big smile on his face, he had to quell his urge to hug her. And looking at her, she seemed apprehensive, maybe even afraid. Concern clouded his thoughts. Was the dog all right? Was this not a routine visit? But he tried to maintain his smile. "Hello, Angie, Lady. Everything all right? You look worried." Immediately, he kneeled down, put the dog's face into his hands, and checked her eyes and her mouth.

"She's fine, Dr. Weiss. We only came in for her annual checkup and titers." Angie shrugged.

"Oh, that's good, then." He looked at her, still concerned, then turned to get his stethoscope and a needle to draw Lady's blood for the titers. Kneeling back down, he put the stethoscope on Lady's heart and listened. Everything sounded perfect. The dog was healthy which was one good thing. But sneaking a quick glance toward Angie, he still thought something might be the matter with her. He drew the blood, prepared it, and then looked at the woman.

Without thinking, he put his hand on her arm. "Are *you* all right? Is the divorce going badly?"

That brought a smile to her lips, albeit a small one. "Yes, I'm"—she hesitated—"fine. Divorce is going fine. I mean, well, it's over. I mean final." She nodded. "Yup, divorce is final, and all is well." She looked at the floor.

238

Dr. Weiss put his hand on her arm again. "You don't look like all is well, if you don't mind my saying."

Breath came out her nose quickly, along with an unhumorous laugh. "Yeah, well, I wasn't really looking forward to coming here today. I didn't want to see you."

"And yet, here you are." His smile spread across his face.

"The only reason I'm here, Dr. Weiss, is because after hours upon hours of researching the perfect vet for Lady, I couldn't find a one. I had one picked out, but she got married and moved out of state. Then I had another one picked out—holistic even—and he had already retired. So that's why I'm here. Believe me, after our conversation last time, I *never* wanted to see you again."

This time, he crossed his arms over his chest and stepped back. "Why? Did I say something that made you think I wasn't a good vet?" He knew what she had meant, but he wanted her to say it.

Angie put her hands on the examining table between them. "Dr. Weiss, you know damn well what I'm talking about!" Her voice was whisper-quiet, but it was obvious it was a yell. "You're *married*!"

He put his hand on Lady's head. "I didn't realize that was a concern to Lady, or that it had anything to do with my ability as a vet."

"It makes a difference to *me*!" She staggered back a step and tears sprang into her eyes.

Dr. Weiss wanted her to say it, but he didn't realize that she would become so emotional. Now he felt bad and wanted to make it up to her. Quickly, he leaned forward and took both of her hands in his. She tried to pull away, but he wouldn't let her. "Look at me, Angie." He could see that she wanted to, but she fought it.

"Please. Look at me." When she looked up, the tears rolled down her face.

"Listen to me," he said. "This morning, my *wife*, who hasn't been a wife to me in many years, told me very succinctly that she was leaving me and moving in with someone else. So, in my book, that means I'm not *technically* married anymore." He released her hands and she didn't pull them away.

"You're not just saying that?"

He brought her hands up to his mouth and kissed each one. "I swear to you that it's the truth." When she broke down with tears flowing down her face, he pulled her around the side of the examining table and wrapped his arms around her. "Listen, you're my last patient. Would you like to go to dinner with me tonight? I was going to celebrate by myself, but now I have two things to celebrate."

She nodded without saying anything, but he could feel that she hugged him tighter.

"And soon, I'd like you to meet my dog, Wolf. I think he'd like to meet you."

"I'd like to meet him, too. I think that he and I will love each other."

He ran his hands down Angela's long hair. "I think so, too, Angie. I think so, too."

As they stood there in a snug embrace, Rolf whispered into her ear, "I have a funny feeling that we finally got it right."

Angelika nodded her head against his chest. "I was thinking the same thing."

Made in the USA
Middletown, DE
05 April 2017